She woke up with the feel of his lips on hers.

What was wrong with her?

Why did she continue to think about Zach in ways that only made her situation worse? As a potential lover, he was totally off-limits. No amount of wishing would make it otherwise.

Her inability to wipe something—well, some*one*—out of her mind when she told herself to was frustrating. And fantasizing about kissing someone when kissing him was the last thing in the world she'd ever be doing was just plain ridiculous.

I will conquer this. Even if it kills me.

And, she thought ruefully, if the unfulfilled, almost painful ache in her body was any indication, it just might.

Dear Reader,

I love Cinderella stories, don't you? From the original story of Cinderella to all the ones that have come after it, they never fail to make me feel good and to put a smile on my face.

Meet Mr. Prince is a Cinderella story, even though Georgie Fairchild is the opposite of the unloved stepsister. Georgie has a fabulous family that includes three beloved sisters, a wonderful job that she loves and a life she considers perfect. She is not looking for Prince Charming. Yet when he comes along, all of Georgie's ideas are turned upside down and her life changes dramatically.

I had a wonderful time writing this book because I loved Georgie from page one. I loved that she's so stubborn and sure of herself, that she is so adamant about not wanting to get married or have children. Nothing is more fun than knowing a character is going to have to eat her words.

I hope you enjoy reading Georgie's story as much as I enjoyed writing it.

Happy reading!

Patricia Kay

MEET
MR. PRINCE

PATRICIA KAY

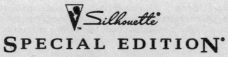

SPECIAL EDITION

Published by Silhouette Books

America's Publisher of Contemporary Romance

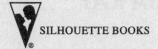

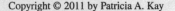

 SILHOUETTE BOOKS

ISBN-13: 978-0-373-65581-6

Recycling programs
for this product may
not exist in your area.

MEET MR. PRINCE

Books by Patricia Kay

Books written as Trisha Alexander

PATRICIA KAY

Formerly writing as Trisha Alexander, Patricia Kay is a *USA TODAY* bestselling author of more than forty-eight novels of contemporary romance and women's fiction. She lives in Houston, Texas. To learn more about her, visit her website at www.patriciakay.com.

This book is dedicated to fellow authors Lois Faye Dyer, Christine Flynn and Allison Leigh. I have loved working with the three of you on this series and look forward to our next adventure together.

Chapter One

Georgianna Hunt Fairchild glared at her mother. "I can't believe you said that."

Cornelia Fairchild, as always, remained unruffled. "Darling Georgie. What I can't believe is that I've somehow managed to upset you."

"I'm not upset. I'm just tired of people trying to interfere in my personal life."

"People? I'm hardly *people*."

Georgie rolled her eyes. "When you start trying to fix me up with every Tom, Dick and Rupert out there, you've joined the ranks of *people!* How many times do I have to tell you *and* my sisters *and* Uncle Harry *and* Alex *and* every other person who might know my name that *I am not interested in getting married*. Period. End of story."

Completely frustrated, Georgie jumped up and began pacing around her mother's living room. "Do you know that the other day *Joanna* invited me to dinner, and when I got there, it wasn't just her and Chick the way I thought it would be, but she'd invited Chick's *brother?*"

Joanna Spinelli was Georgie's former college roommate and her BFF. She was currently having a torrid romance with Chick London, her boss—big mistake, Georgie thought, mixing her work life with her personal life, as nothing good could come of it—and now she seemed to want everyone else to enter the same besotted state.

"What was so wrong with that?" Cornelia asked.

"Look, Chick's brother is nice enough, but it was obvious that Joanna was trying to fix me up with him! Dammit, I don't *want* to be fixed up with anyone, and she *knows* that."

"Please don't swear, Georgie. It's very unladylike."

"Sorry. But honestly, Joanna of all people should know better. And then *Bobbie* called and got on my case." Bobbie was the youngest of the four Fairchild sisters, and she was practically still on her honeymoon and wild about her new husband. In fact, all of Georgie's sisters seemed to be wildly in love...or lust, although they would say they had found their soul mates. Georgie had yet to be convinced that such a thing existed.

"Your sisters love you, Georgie," her mother said softly. "And so does Joanna."

"I know they do, Mom, but doesn't that mean they should listen to me once in a while? I listen to them." Georgie ignored the little voice of her conscience that said she didn't *always* listen to them.

Cornelia shook her head sadly. "Oh, all right, Georgie, have it your own way. But just wait. One of these days you'll be a forty-something woman with no husband, no children and no prospects. *Then* let's see how you feel!

"Besides, I was not trying to fix you up," she added. "Trust me, I've learned my lesson in that area. All I said was Josie Wilcox's nephew is staying with her while he's in Seattle on business and he's at loose ends, and from what she's said about him, he sounds as if you two might have a lot in common."

"You know, Mom, first of all—no offense against you, but I barely know Josie Wilcox and from what I do know of her, I have no desire to meet her nephew. Second of all, I have a long way to go until I'm forty-something, considering I've just barely turned thirty. And last of all, don't you remember what that survey showed? The one where they interviewed married men, single men, married women and single women?"

Her mother said nothing, simply picked up her mug of tea and sipped. Her thoughtful eyes studied Georgie over the rim of the cup.

"Well, I do," Georgie said. "That survey found—and I believe it—that the happiest people are, number one, married men, and, number two, single *women*. And the *un*happiest people are married women!"

"Oh, for heaven's sake, Georgie. Anyone can prove anything with a survey. Everyone knows that surveys are skewed by all kinds of things. Why, I know any number of happily married women."

Georgie sighed. "I don't want to argue with you. Try to understand, okay? I'm happy the way I am. Unlike your other daughters, I really don't want to get married. I mean, what's the point if you don't want children? I know that just goes against everything you believe, but I'm being honest with myself, and I don't think I'm cut out to be a mother. Can't you respect that?"

Her mother glanced out the windows of her recently renovated porch, which was now a sunroom and extension of the living room. Georgie's gaze followed. The view of Puget Sound from the family's hilltop home in Queen Anne—one of Georgie's favorite areas of Seattle—was a sight she had never tired of. Today could have been a day in high summer instead of January: The sun was shining and the water sparkled as if dusted by thousands of diamonds. Maybe one day she, too, would have a home like this, but Georgie intended to pay for every last brick with money *she* earned. Instead of sublimating her goals for a husband's. Instead of spending her days ferrying spoiled and overindulged kids to soccer games and skating lessons. Instead of her giving up her independence and freedom. She was sorry if her decisions had made her mother unhappy, but this was *her* life, not her mother's!

Cornelia took her time before answering. "If I thought you wouldn't deeply regret this decision one day, I *would* respect it, Georgie. But darling, I just don't think you understand how you'll feel when you're older and your childbearing days are over." Turning back to Georgie, her green eyes—the same color as Georgie's—were filled with love. "I've seen it all too often. Think about your cousin Sophie."

Sophie Fairchild Jamison was the only daughter of Georgie's father's older brother Franklin. Sophie had married late and had desperately been trying to have a child the past few years, with no success.

"I'm not Sophie. I have a demanding job I love, a wonderful family and tons of friends, and if I ever feel the need for a child of my own, I'll adopt. God knows there are millions of children all over the world who desperately need someone to love them." Georgie had seen too many of them in her work for the Hunt Foundation. Many nights her dreams were haunted by their sad eyes.

"Yes, I know. But you could do that, too, you know." Now it was Cornelia's turn to sigh. "All right, Georgie. I'll quit 'bugging' you, as you've so inelegantly expressed it. And I'll just pray you won't regret this decision some day."

"Thank you, Mother." Now that she'd won her point, Georgie could afford to be magnanimous. She walked to her mother's chair and knelt before her. "You know I love you, don't you? And that I'm grateful for everything you've sacrificed for us? We can agree to disagree about this one thing, can't we?"

Her mother smiled. "Yes, but that doesn't mean I won't continue to worry about you."

Georgie raised herself up and kissed her mother's still-smooth cheek. "I know. I guess I can't ask for miracles." Then she grinned. "Although if anyone can accomplish miracles, it's you."

"Look who's talking, Miss I-Finished-College-in-Three-Years-and-Got-My-Master's-in-Less-than-Two.'"

Although Georgie had never had problems with self-confidence, sometimes her mother's praise and her sisters' admiration made her uncomfortable. She was not exceptional or brilliant, and she kept trying to tell them so. She just knew what she wanted, she worked hard and she didn't waste her time. If she made a bad decision, the moment she realized it was bad, she rectified it. Her sisters were all hard workers, too, but some of them lacked confidence and hesitated before making changes. It was a mystery to Georgie that the four them, so close in age, all born to the very same mother and father, could be so different.

Take Tommi, for instance. The only place she seemed to feel completely sure of herself was in the kitchen.

"So what's on your agenda now?" her mother asked. "Has Alex made any decision about where you'll go next?"

Georgie shook her head. "God, I hope so. We're meeting for lunch tomorrow. Aside from anything else, it'll be nice to see him again."

Her mother frowned. "I thought you were working at Alex's office the past couple of weeks while waiting for a new assignment."

"Not *at* the office. I'm doing research for him at home. But I'll sure be glad to get back into the field. I like research, but not *that* much."

Despite this minor complaint, Georgie loved her job, loved that Alex allowed her to have a say in what she did and where she did it. Since coming to work for him at the Hunt Foundation nineteen months earlier, Georgie had been happier than she'd ever been in her entire life.

Alex was a dream boss. One of the things about him she liked most was that he treated all his employees with consideration and respect. P.J., his wife, was one lucky woman. In fact, if Georgie ever found a man like Alex, she might even change her mind about getting married.

"What're you smiling about?" her mother asked.

Georgie started. She'd forgotten her mother was sitting there. Not a good idea. Her mother was too sharp. She had an uncanny ability to almost read a person's mind, to the chagrin of all her daughters. "Oh, nothing. Just thinking how happy I'll be to get busy again."

Georgie had come home from the Sudan right before

the Christmas holiday had begun and had now been on hiatus more than three weeks. She'd told Alex she didn't need that much time off. After all, she had no husband, children or pets to worry about. And although she was the newly proud owner of a small, loft-type condo in near downtown Belltown, the maid service and condo maintenance she paid for took excellent care of her property when she was away.

"Well," her mother said, "I hope, if he's sending you out to the field again, he sends you somewhere peaceful this time. It worries me when you go into countries where there's so much civil unrest."

"You know Alex would never put me in danger."

Cornelia raised her eyebrows. "Afghanistan is terribly dangerous. And so was Burundi. And even the Sudan."

"I was never in danger in any of those places." But Georgie mentally crossed her fingers, because she wasn't telling her mother the entire truth. Sure, she'd been in supposedly protected zones in those countries, and in all cases she'd been accompanied by representatives from the UN, along with a security detail, but still…no one was ever completely safe surrounded by warring factions, and she'd had one or two close—and scary—calls.

Cornelia nodded, but Georgie knew she wasn't convinced. Giving her mother another kiss, she said, "I've gotta run, Mom. I'm getting my hair trimmed. My appointment's at three o'clock."

"Phone me tomorrow?" her mother said as she walked Georgie to the door.

"Why? So you can call Alex and yell at him if you don't like where he's sending me next?" teased Georgie.

Her mother laughed. "Don't think I wouldn't."

"Oh, I *know* you would." And the worst part was, Alex would probably listen. Sometimes Georgie despaired of ever leading a totally independent life. But that's what she got for taking a job with someone so closely intertwined with her family. Although she and Alex Hunt referred to each other as cousins, they were not really related. Their fathers had been best friends as kids, and as young men they'd co-founded a company that eventually became HuntCom.

Of course, the company's huge success came years after George Fairchild's death, so neither he nor Cornelia had benefitted financially the way Harry Hunt, Alex's father, had. It wasn't for lack of trying on Harry's part, though. Harry Hunt wasn't perfect, but he was nothing if not generous to the people he loved. And George Fairchild's wife and daughters were high up on that list. Harry had tried everything he could think of to give Cornelia money, and she had thwarted every attempt. He *had* managed to gift each of her daughters with $100,000 upon their high-school graduation, along with an honorary seat on the HuntCom board. Furious, Cornelia had refused to talk to him for months afterward.

Cornelia was proud. She wasn't willing to take money she didn't feel she deserved, no matter how much she could have used the help at the time. And the same applied to her daughters.

Georgie admired her mother more than just about anyone. How many women would have had guts enough and strength enough to hold their heads high after finding out, after his death, that the husband they'd trusted had gambled away every bit of their life's savings, including their stock in HuntCom? How many women would refuse to take the easy way out that had been offered by Harry Hunt? Not many, Georgie thought.

Cornelia Phillips Fairchild hadn't wasted a whole lot of time feeling sorry for herself, either. She'd sold the family home, the one asset George Fairchild had not been able to touch, because it belonged to Cornelia outright—her inheritance from the maternal grandmother she'd been named for. She'd bought the much smaller Craftsman-style bungalow in Queen Anne that she still lived in, and she'd taken a job as secretary at the small private girls' school where her daughters were enrolled. In that way, with what she got for the girls in Social Security, what remained from the sale of the big house and her small salary supplementing free tuition for the girls, she was able to keep their lives as close to normal as possible.

Yes, her mother was a remarkable woman, and Georgie thought the world of her. Even so, she mused as she drove away from the family home, she was no longer a child who needed her mother's guidance, especially when it came to her love life…or lack thereof.

Georgie hoped they'd settled that subject today and that Cornelia wouldn't be raising it again. Then she grinned. Of course her mother would raise it again. Her mother wasn't the type to give up easily.

Well, I'm not, either. No one was going to talk her into doing anything she didn't want to do—absolutely no one.

Zachary Prince was ready for the weekend to begin. Although he really liked his job, today he was tired of being cooped up in the office, tired of all the problems associated with too much work and too few people to do it since his assistant had quit, and he just wanted to go home and spend time with his children.

He often felt guilty because he didn't need to work. He could stay home and be with the kids full-time. After all, he didn't need the money. He and his twin sister, Sabrina, had inherited a stock portfolio worth many millions from their grandfather, McKinley. But Zach liked his work as director of the New York office of the Hunt Foundation. And he was wise enough to know that as much as he loved his children, he would go crazy at home all day, especially now that his two oldest, Katie and Jeremy, were in school.

He was so lost in his thoughts that he jumped when his phone buzzed. The CID showed Alex Hunt's name.

"Hey, Alex."

"Hey, Zach. I've got some good news for you. I think I'll be able to send some help your way."

"Really? Who? Anybody I know?"

"She works for me, but you haven't met her because she's been in the field the past year and a half. Her name is Georgianna Fairchild."

Fairchild. Weren't the Fairchilds close friends of the Hunts? And weren't some of them on the HuntCom board? No matter how badly Zach needed help in the New York office, he didn't think having a friend of the Hunt family there was a great idea. But before he could think of a tactful way to say so, Alex continued talking.

"In addition to her experience in the field, Georgie's a whiz at research. She can take over that part of the work easily…and anything else you want her to do. You can trust her, Zach. She's totally dependable…and she's got good judgment. I think she'll be a real asset to you."

Because he couldn't think of any other rejoinder,

Zach just said, "She does sound good. Um, when is she coming?"

"I haven't discussed this with her yet, so I don't want to commit until I do. We're having lunch tomorrow and we'll talk about it. I need her here at least another week, and since this will be different from the kinds of assignments she's had in the past, in that she'll be staying in New York until we can find a permanent assistant for you, she may need more time after that to make arrangements. For now, let's say she'll be there by the fifteenth of next month."

Zach listened as Alex continued to extol the virtues of Georgie Fairchild, but despite her vaunted capabilities, Zach had a bad feeling about this. No matter what Alex said, Zach didn't think having a Hunt family friend on staff was a good idea. What if they didn't like each other? What if she were one of those strong-willed women who thought she knew everything and didn't take orders well?

After they hung up, Zach sat there, staring into space and thinking. And the more he thought, the more uneasy he felt. Was it possible that Alex was sending this Fairchild woman to New York to spy on him?

Maybe Alex was unhappy with the way things were going in New York. Maybe he'd decided he'd made a mistake when he'd hired Zach, especially considering the special deal Zach had negotiated. Maybe he didn't think Zach was carrying his weight. But hell, if that were the case, why didn't Alex just say so? Zach had always believed Alex was a straight shooter, that he'd never do anything underhanded.

But maybe Zach had been wrong.

He guessed only time would tell.

Time, and this Georgie Fairchild.

Chapter Two

Georgie always loved lunching with Alex. It used to be the highlight of her week during the brief period she'd worked in downtown Seattle. Lord, she'd hated that first job at the ad agency. Why she'd taken it, she still couldn't fathom. But it had served its purpose because she'd quickly realized she wasn't cut out for the business world and she'd gone back to school and gotten her master's in sociology.

Once she had that degree in hand, she'd gone to work for a large women's hospital. Idealistic when she began, four years later she was burned out. One day she'd admitted to Alex that her job had become depressing and that most days she felt she was spinning her wheels and getting nowhere.

"My hands are tied by lack of money and facilities," she'd said, "And it's getting worse all the time. Besides, I really want to work with kids. I may not think I'd make a good mother, but I still prefer being around kids to being around most adults. Kids are honest, and they appreciate everything you do for them. I want to do something that makes me feel as if I'm really making a difference."

"Then," Alex had said, "it's time for you to come to work for the foundation."

Georgie couldn't believe how much she loved the work she did now. Her job satisfied every part of her. She felt she'd finally found her niche in life. She loved the travel, she loved learning about different peoples and their culture, she loved the children she met and helped and she didn't even mind the fundraising because she was asking for money for a cause she believed in passionately. But most of all, she loved that she *was* making a difference. Everything about her work was rewarding.

Of course, there was still the problem of money. Trouble is, there was never enough money for all the things that needed doing. But that was minor compared to the way she'd felt before coming to work at the foundation.

So today, in addition to the pleasure of spending some private time with Alex—they hadn't seen much of each other since she'd been home, even though she'd been working at the foundation office while waiting to go back into the field—she also had a new assignment to look forward to. She could hardly wait to find out where it would be. Haiti? Indonesia? Ethiopia?

They were lunching at Wild Ginger, one of her favorite places to eat in Seattle. When Georgie arrived, Alex was already there and had secured a window table, a feat in itself at the popular restaurant. Georgie couldn't help smiling as she approached the table. Alex stood to give her a kiss on the cheek, and once again, she thought how handsome he was. Tall and slender, with dark hair and dark brown eyes, he was a man who attracted admiring looks wherever he went. And when he smiled! Well, even Georgie wasn't immune to those dimples. But Alex was well and truly taken, and even if he hadn't been, he was too much like real family, almost the brother she'd never had.

"You're looking mighty sharp today," he said once she was settled across from him.

Georgie grinned. Alex knew she would have scoffed if he'd said "pretty" because she wasn't pretty, and she knew it. The term *pretty* was for cute little cheerleader types, not for five-ten Amazons. "Sharp as in brilliant, or sharp as in chic?"

He laughed. "I'm pretty sure the safest answer is 'both.'"

She grinned. "I can see *you're* as sharp as ever, too."

They continued the lighthearted banter while they studied the menu. Georgie finally tossed her menu aside. There was really no point in looking at it. She always ordered the same thing: the pot stickers—their pot stickers were to die for—and the Spice Trader's Beef. Alex was more adventurous and always tried something different. Today his choices were the Buddha Roll and the Nonya Noodles.

That settled, Georgie finally asked the question she'd been dying to ask. "Well? Don't keep me in suspense. Have you finally got another field assignment for me?"

"What? We're not keeping you busy enough at the office?"

"Alex…"

"Haven't you enjoyed being around for your sister's wedding and all the holiday stuff?"

She rolled her eyes. "Alex, stop teasing me."

His smile said he was pleased with himself. "You'll be going somewhere very different from past assignments."

"Really? That sounds intriguing. Where?"

Alex waited a heartbeat, then said, "New York."

Georgie's smile faded. "New York? You mean…New York City?"

"Yes, our New York office."

"But…why?" Georgie told herself not to get upset.

"Because Zachary Prince, the director of the New York office, is in a bind right now. His assistant quit a month ago and we've had no luck replacing him. We've had a lot of candidates, but no one qualified or experienced enough to be a real asset. I don't want to hire someone just to hire someone. What we do out of New York is too important. That's why I thought of you."

"But, Alex, that's not what I do, I don't work in an *office,* and I don't want to waste—"

He held up his hand. "Wait. Hear me out before you say you don't want the assignment."

Georgie made a face.

"This is only temporary, Georgie. Just until we can find a permanent replacement. Both Zach and I intend to keep looking, but in the meantime—as soon as you can wind things up here—you're perfect for the job. You don't need any training, and you can be an immediate help to Zach, which is a huge plus. And just because you're working out of the office doesn't mean you won't go into the field. In fact, being Zach's assistant means you'll get plenty of chances to look into possible beneficiaries of the Hunt Foundation—the only difference being that those beneficiaries will mostly be in the eastern part of the U.S. Wouldn't you like to go to Appalachia?"

"Well, of course, I'd like to go to Appalachia, but—"

"But what?"

"I like doing evaluations. That's what I'm good at."

"I know that. It's one of the big reasons you're so perfect for this job. Zach tells me the pile of requests for assistance is stacking up faster than they can look at them."

"You're saying I'll still get to do the evaluations and make recommendations?" Georgie knew she sounded skeptical. Shoot, she *was* skeptical. In her experience, assistants didn't get the interesting jobs. They got the jobs the directors didn't want to do themselves, probably involving tons of paperwork, which Georgie despised. Suddenly a new thought struck her. "Did my mother put you up to this?"

"Put me up to what?"

"Sending me to New York."

"Georgie, come on…don't be paranoid."

"I'm not being paranoid. I know my mother. If she had gotten even an inkling about what happened in Burundi, I know she'd have been on the phone to you in an instant."

"I haven't talked to your mother. She knows nothing about this assignment."

"You're sure." But even as she said it, she could see from Alex's expression that he was telling her the truth.

She sank back in her chair, her shoulders slumping.

"Come on, Georgie. Cheer up. This assignment is going to be good for you. Good for all of us." When she didn't answer, Alex added softly, "Have I ever steered you wrong?"

It killed her to say it, but she finally said, "No."

Alex started to say something else but quit because their waiter had brought their food. When he left them alone again, Georgie sighed and said, "You're sure this assignment is only temporary?"

Alex raised his right hand. "I swear, this is absolutely temporary. And the more you can do to relieve Zach, the more time he'll have to find a replacement for you." Then came the kicker. "If you do this for me, Georgie, I'll owe you."

Georgie wished she could say no. She knew if she adamantly refused to go to New York, Alex wouldn't force her. But how could she? Alex was her boss and her friend. He'd never before asked for a favor. And she owed him big time, even though he was too nice to remind her of that fact.

"Oh, all right, Alex. You win." She picked up her chopsticks. "How soon do you want me to be there?"

Cornelia's cell phone vibrated from the depths of her handbag as she walked toward the south entrance of Nordstrom. She managed to find the phone before the call went to voice mail and saw from the display that it was Harry calling. She felt like ignoring the call, but a mixture of curiosity and the certain knowledge that Harry Hunt, accustomed as he was to people leaping when he said, "Jump," would just keep trying until she answered trumped her desire to continue making a statement by avoiding him.

Sighing, she pressed the talk icon. "Hello, Harry."

"Corny, I'm glad I caught you."

"Yes, well, I'm just on my way into Nordstrom." She kept her voice deliberately cool.

"Then I won't keep you long. I just wondered if my favorite gal in the entire world would do me the honor of accompanying me to a dinner next Saturday night."

Cornelia could have said a lot of things in response to his "favorite gal" comment, but she decided it was wiser not to. Why open that can of worms? Especially when nothing ever changed. "What kind of dinner?" she hedged.

"Oh, I'm getting some award from the Software Society of America. The dinner's being held at the Fairmont, and you know how I hate these black-tie things. But it'd be bearable if you'd come with me." He chuckled. "Make that rubber chicken go down a lot easier."

I should say no. I should say I'm tired of being an also-ran with you. I should say go find yourself another one of your models or actresses to take. I should say I already have a date.

But she didn't think Harry knew about her fledgling relationship with Greg Berger, the golf pro at the club, and Cornelia wasn't sure she wanted him to know. She could just imagine what he'd have to say about her dating a much younger man. Of course, every single one of Harry's four wives had been considerably younger than *him*. But that was different, wasn't it? Cornelia gritted her teeth. Just thinking about Harry's former wives and the double standard about age stiffened her resolve. "I don't think I can, Harry."

"Don't *think* you can?"

"I believe I have another engagement." Despite everything, she couldn't bring herself to outright lie to him. "I'll have to check my calendar after I get home."

"If you have another engagement, break it. I really want you to be with me at that dinner, Corny."

"I—" *Where's your backbone? Just say no.*

"Please, Corny. I haven't seen nearly enough of you lately."

"And whose fault is that?" she retorted before she could stop herself.

"I realize it *is* my fault, but I'm trying to rectify that. C'mon, say you'll go. I really want to see you."

Cornelia could feel herself weakening, and it infuriated her. Why did she find it so hard to refuse him? He was entirely too sure of himself. Break it, indeed! And yet, despite all this, she sighed and said, "Oh, all right, Harry. I'll go with you."

"That's my girl. We'll pick you up at seven."

Cornelia shook her head as she disconnected the call. She was spineless. Yet she couldn't help remembering a night long ago when she had said no to Harry. And who knows how different all their lives might have been if she'd said yes instead.

We were too young, and I was afraid. And when I was finally ready to say yes, it was too late. He'd moved on with wife number one, and then George and I fell in love. After that, all of our lives continued in different directions from the way I'd first imagined they'd go.

She was so lost in the memory of that fateful night when she was only seventeen, a memory she rarely indulged, that she very nearly ran into a young mother exiting Nordstrom while juggling a toddler, a big black umbrella and several packages.

"Sorry," Cornelia apologized, holding the door open for her.

"No problem," the harried young woman said.

No problem, Cornelia thought, ducking inside to

avoid having to open her own umbrella, for it had just begun to rain. The young woman was right. Some things weren't worth getting rattled over.

I must stop thinking about the past. What happened, happened. And despite Harry's cluelessness and Georgie's stubbornness and my occasional aches and pains, I have no real problems. My life turned out the way it was supposed to turn out.

Her momentary twinge of nostalgia and regret evaporated as she walked briskly into the store.

"Daddeeeee!"

Zach grinned as Emma, his three-year-old, raced down the hall and launched herself at him as he entered their spacious eleventh-floor apartment near Lincoln Center. Was there any feeling as wonderful as this? he thought as he lifted her up and she twined her dimpled arms around his neck.

"Hello, sweetness," he murmured.

"Mr. Prince. You're home early." This observation came from Fanny, his fifty-something housekeeper, who had followed Emma into the foyer.

Zach kissed his daughter, relishing the sweet, little-girl smell and the softness of her skin. "I decided everything on my desk could wait till Monday."

It had taken nearly two years for him to stop dreading that first few minutes after arriving home, minutes in which the awareness of Jenny's absence would strike him yet again, minutes when he'd thought the hollow ache in the vicinity of his heart would never go away. But he was finally adjusting to the fact that she was gone, that cancer had taken his beloved wife at a too-young age and he had been left to raise their three children alone.

He knew he would always treasure the memory of Jenny and he would always miss her, but now he also knew he was going to be okay, because he was finally beginning to think about the future instead of constantly mourning the past.

"And how was your day?" Fanny asked. Her hazel eyes were warm as they studied him.

What would he do without Fanny? He couldn't even imagine. She was more than a housekeeper, even though that's how they both referred to her. In many ways, she reminded him of his mother in the manner that she looked after him and his children.

"It was good," he said. "Got a lot done. But I sure am glad to be home. Where are the other two?" Glancing at the grandfather clock that graced the foyer, he saw it was a few minutes before five. Katie, his ten-year-old, and Jeremy, seven, normally were home from school by four.

"Katie's at Madison Werner's house. They're working on a science project together. She'll be home at six-thirty. And your sister came by to take Jeremy skating. She said she'd have him back by nine."

"I wanted to go skating," Emma said, her blue eyes clouding. "But Jeremy said I'm too little! I'm *not* too little, Daddy." Her voice rose in volume with each word.

Sensing a full-blown tantrum brewing, Zach said, "Of course you're not too little, sweetheart. We'll go skating Sunday afternoon. How's that?"

"To Rocky Center."

"This time I think we'll go to the park, honey. The rink at Rockefeller Center is too crowded."

Emma's frown deepened. "I don't care! I wanna go to Rocky Center."

Suppressing a grin, Zach lowered his daughter to

the floor. "Tell you what, pumpkin, we'll decide on Sunday."

"I'm not a pumpkin!"

Zach could no longer prevent a smile. "You're *my* pumpkin."

Not to be sidetracked from her grievance, Emma put her hands on her hips and deepened her frown. "Jeremy can't go skating with us. Just girls."

"Today was just-boys day," Fanny explained *sotto voce*.

Zach knew without further explanation that Sabrina had probably been trying to make Emma feel better after Jeremy's taunt about her being too little, so she'd made the remark about boys only. Zach didn't blame his twin for not wanting to take Emma along today. Sabrina's Tommy was eight, and he and Jeremy were best buddies. Emma's presence would have put a damper on their fun together. Besides, his youngest daughter had to learn she couldn't do everything her older siblings did.

"You know," Zach said carefully, "I think it would be more fun for all of us to go skating on Sunday. Then we can show Jeremy just how big you are. Wouldn't you like that?"

Emma stamped her foot. "No! I don't want Jeremy to go." She pronounced his name *Jare-mee*, with two syllables.

Man, she wasn't going to give an inch. "Yes, you've made that very clear," he said dryly. Well, he'd just have to hope she had a short memory, because skating was one thing they could all do together as a family. And because Emma *was* so young, it was tough to find activities that worked for everyone.

"I hate Jeremy," she muttered. "He's mean."

"Emma…"

His youngest glared at him.

"Jeremy is your brother. You don't hate him. You're mad at him right now, and that's okay. You can be mad if you want to be. But I don't want to hear you saying you hate him. I don't want to hear you saying you hate anyone. We don't hate people in this house."

For a moment, Zach was afraid she would defy him and say it again. She certainly looked like she wanted to. And then what would he do? Of his three children, Emma was the most stubborn and the most difficult to sway. *Father Bested by Three-Year-Old,* he thought, seeing the headline in his mind.

Why didn't anyone tell you how hard it was to be a parent? He wished he'd understood just how hard while Jenny was still alive, because he should have gotten down on his knees and thanked her every single day for the wonderful job she was doing.

"Mr. Prince?"

Zach had almost forgotten Fanny was still standing there.

"Mr. Hunt called a few minutes ago. I put the message on the desk in your study."

Lured by Fanny's offer to make her hot chocolate with marshmallows, Emma trotted off after the housekeeper, and Zach headed into his home office.

Five minutes later, he had Alex Hunt on the line.

"Just wanted you to know I had lunch with Georgie Fairchild today, and she'll report to work for you on the seventh."

Zach glanced at his calendar. "That's sooner than you thought."

"She wanted to get going even sooner," Alex continued. "But we compromised. She'll be staying at the corporate apartment in New York, at least initially. If it turns out she's going to be in there more than a month or two, then we'll see about making other arrangements."

"Hell, Alex, I sure hope it doesn't take more than a month to find a permanent assistant." The last thing Zach wanted was for this Fairchild woman to be hanging over him for weeks on end.

"I hope not, either, but you never know. It's better to be prepared."

Zach stifled the urge to say some of the things he'd been thinking. Instead, he said, "Yeah, I guess you're right. Okay. I'll have Deborah make sure everything at the apartment is in order."

Deborah Zelinsky was Zach's office manager and, even though the corporate apartment didn't technically fall under the jurisdiction of the foundation, she was always more than happy to make sure the unit was ready for a visiting dignitary or prospective contributor.

"Thanks, Zach. I think Georgie is going to be a great addition to your team. I know the two of you will get along like a house afire."

After they'd hung up, Zach sat thinking for a long moment. He still wished he'd said something to Alex about his doubts. And yet, how could he, especially without saying what had prompted those doubts? It wasn't like he could have come right out and said, *Hey, Alex, are you unhappy with me? Is that why you're sending a spy to New York?*

Oh, hell, he had to stop thinking about this. For this weekend, at least, he needed to put Georgie Fairchild and anything else connected to the office out of his mind. Time enough to think about work issues again on Monday.

In the meantime, he'd rather think about Emma, who was a lot more fun, and a lot more important to him, than anything—or anyone—connected with his job could ever be.

"Fanny," he called as he headed for the kitchen. "Did you make enough hot chocolate for me?"

Chapter Three

Georgie didn't believe in spending a lot of time packing. Most of the time, she just threw clothes into her trusty old duffel bag on wheels and figured what she didn't have she would simply go without. And in this case—preparing for an assignment in New York—she could certainly buy anything she needed.

Still…it was winter, and New York was a lot colder than Seattle. Looking at the Weather Channel's website, she saw that the median temperature this month was hovering around forty degrees. Just her luck. If she *had* to go to New York, couldn't Alex at least have sent her in the spring? Or in the fall, which Georgie had been told was probably the most attractive time of the year in Manhattan?

She eyed the clothing she'd piled on her bed. She'd thrown her down parka in the mix and the boots she'd bought last winter in preparation for her trip to Korea.

But she didn't own a nice winter coat, certainly nothing suitable for meeting with potential donors and grant recipients, plus it wouldn't have fit into the duffel even if she did own one. So she'd definitely have to buy a coat when she got to New York.

"Oh, shoot. I don't want to do this."

Even as she muttered the words, she knew she was wasting time and energy on her negative feelings about this assignment. And that was unlike her. What was it about going to New York that was so bad? She'd never been there before, and she'd always wanted to visit. *Yeah, but this isn't a visit.* Still, she'd agreed, and she couldn't change that now. And Alex had promised her time there would only be temporary.

If all went well, they'd find a permanent assistant for Zachary Prince quickly, and Georgie wouldn't have to stay long at all. And yet…she couldn't help thinking there must be some reason other than what Alex had given her about why they hadn't yet been able to find an assistant. Was Zachary Prince difficult to work with? Maybe he was a pain in the butt and Alex hadn't wanted to say so.

Then she told herself she was doing exactly what Alex had told her not to do. She was being paranoid. Granted, this time her paranoia had nothing to do with her mother, but still…

Lecturing herself to stop borrowing trouble and to think positive, she continued packing. She was almost finished when her cell phone, playing Chris Brown's "Forever," sounded from where she'd placed it on her dresser. The song signaled Joanna calling.

"How's my BFF today?" Georgie said by way of greeting.

"Exhausted."

"What's the problem?"

"Too busy, too little time." Joanna was a struggling fashion designer in the Seattle area, and she was always racing to beat a deadline.

"What else is new?" Georgie abandoned the packing and walked over to the window overlooking the parklike grounds adjacent to her condominium. Below she saw a young couple walking with their arms around each other.

"Nothing, really. Just wanted to see how things were going with you. How was the party last night?" Joanna was referring to Frankie's engagement party to Eli Wolf.

"It was really nice."

"And what about Thursday's farewell lunch with your mother?"

"I enjoyed it. At least this time Mom wasn't upset. At least, not with me."

"Who was she upset with?"

"Uncle Harry."

"What's the poor guy done now?"

"It's not what he's done, it's what he hasn't done." Georgie was still amazed at what her mother had revealed right before Christmas. "Joanna, remember when I told you what my mother told me and my sisters? About Uncle Harry and how she'd once had a thing for him? She made it sound like that was in the distant past, but I think she might really be in love with him."

"Did she say that?"

"She didn't have to say it. She was talking about him and some dinner he'd taken her to, and all of a sudden it seemed so obvious I couldn't believe I hadn't realized it before."

"I thought he was more like her brother or something. Didn't you tell me she and your dad and Harry Hunt were like The three Musketeers when they were young? And she picked your dad."

Joanna didn't have to say what Harry had done. They both knew the story. Harry had picked one gorgeous model or actress after another, gold diggers all—at least, in his estimation. Each short-lived marriage had produced one son, and Harry Hunt had gotten sole custody of each of them.

"That's what we all thought," Georgie said. "But maybe we don't know the whole story."

"You mean you think she's always loved Harry? And not your dad?"

"No, I don't believe *that*. I think she loved my dad. But maybe she loved Uncle Harry first. Or maybe… after Dad died…"

"Did you ask her about her feelings yesterday?"

"Good grief, no. You know how private my mother is. Besides, it wasn't like she'd said anything directly. And, I don't know, I felt funny about it. Like maybe it was none of my business."

"Wow," Joanna said, amusement in her voice. "I think that's the first time since I met you that you thought something wasn't your business."

"Oh, stuff it," Georgie said, laughing. But she knew Joanna wasn't far wrong.

"You know," Joanna said, "maybe this explains why Harry got so weird about your mother dating that golf pro from the club."

"You're probably right. Here I thought he was just worried because the guy's so much younger than my mother. But maybe he was actually jealous!"

"It's possible. I know Chick can't stand it when I even *look* at anyone else."

Georgie nodded, even though Joanna couldn't see her. "It all makes sense now. There's got to be some kind of history here, something my sisters and I never suspected."

"Oh, Georgie. It's terribly romantic, isn't it? Maybe they've been pining for each other for years. I know! Why don't you and your sisters turn the tables on them and try to get them together? I mean, they were trying their darnedest to fix you guys up. Why not fix *them* up, because, Lord knows, if you don't, they might never get it right."

Georgie laughed. "It would serve them right, wouldn't it? But think about it. What could we actually do? It's not like we can plop them down on a desert island or something."

"No, but you can maybe nudge them along a bit."

"I'm afraid my sisters will have to do the nudging, 'cause I'll be in New York." Glancing at the digital alarm sitting on her bedside table, she added, "Speaking of, I'd better get a move on. My flight leaves at noon, and I still have to finish packing and get a shower."

"Okay, I'll let you go. Safe trip."

"Thanks." After promising to call or text Joanna as soon as she hit LaGuardia, they said goodbye.

Fifteen minutes later, duffel packed, laptop and cell phone charging, Georgie headed for the shower.

Katie, Zach's ten-year-old, kept Zach up half the night with a sore throat and a fever. On any other day, even if he had work stacked to the ceiling, Zach would have taken the morning off—maybe even the entire day—and taken his daughter to the doctor himself. But today was the day Georgie Fairchild was to report to work, so he reluctantly agreed that Fanny could take Katie to see their pediatrician.

"Don't worry, Mr. Prince. She'll be fine. I'll call you after we've seen Dr. Noble."

But Zach knew he would worry. Worse, he'd feel guilty all day. He should be the one taking care of Katie, not Fanny. As he had so often since Jenny died, he thought about how little consideration he'd ever given to the plight of single parents. But that was before, and this was now. Now he was a single parent himself. And he was fortunate. He had money, and when he couldn't be here, he could afford the best care possible for his children. And yet he still felt guilty when he couldn't do the things Jenny had done.

Some days he felt he was incredibly selfish—working when he didn't have to. And yet everyone needed some kind of work. Worthwhile work was important. He wanted to set that example for his children, even as he wanted to be with them as much as possible.

He was still mulling over his ever-present, unsolvable dilemma as he wearily headed to the office.

Always begin the way you mean to continue. Georgie thought of her mother's advice, given so often over the years, as she dressed for her first day in the New York office.

Good thing she'd arrived in the city a few days early. She'd quickly discovered her ideas of what New York women wear were wrong. First of all, she didn't own anywhere near enough black. Second, she needed better walking boots that she could actually wear to the office—ones that wouldn't be ruined by dirty snow and slush—because New York was definitely a walking city, which she actually liked.

Now, after a couple of necessary shopping trips, she felt as if she fit in. At least she wouldn't look like a tourist.

She'd also scoped out the location of the Hunt Foundation's New York office (only a couple of blocks away from the corporate apartment), the closest Starbucks (after all, she was a Seattle girl, and if she couldn't have her daily fix of her sister Bobbie's brew, she'd take theirs) and the best place to buy tickets to hear classical musicians she admired (this she was still investigating).

Now she was armed and ready to meet her new boss.

Dressed in black wool pants, her new black boots, businesslike white blouse, lightweight black cardigan and a good-looking black wool coat she'd bought on sale at Bloomingdale's, she left the apartment at 8:25, even though supposedly the office didn't open for business until nine. Why so late? she wondered. Seattle offices started their workday at eight. Did a nine o'clock start have something to do with being on Eastern Time? She guessed it didn't really matter. There was a Starbucks conveniently close by; she'd just duck in there and get a skinny latte.

Latte in hand, she arrived at the foundation office eight minutes before nine, at the same time an attractive redhead was unlocking the door. The redhead looked up. "Hi. Can I help you?"

"I'm Georgie Fairchild. I—"

"Oh, yes, of course. We're expecting you. I'm Deborah Zelinsky, the office manager here." She pulled off a wool glove and stuck out her right hand. "C'mon in.

I generally get here earlier, but my son woke up with a stomachache and, well, you know…"

Georgie nodded, although she really didn't know… and didn't want to know what it must be like to be both mother and employee. She felt capable of many things, but juggling two such important roles seemed to her to be the ultimate in self-sacrifice. She had nothing but admiration for working mothers—for *all* mothers— but was glad she'd realized early on that role wasn't for her.

Following Deborah into the office, Georgie quickly saw it wasn't a fancy place. Not that she'd expected it to be. Most foundations, even well-funded ones, didn't waste money on frills. And if they *did,* then they were suspect in Georgie's eyes.

Substance over flash, that was Georgie's credo.

Deborah dumped her handbag and a paper sack onto a desk in the outer office and gestured to a group of chairs against the wall. "Have a seat. Let me get things turned on and organized, then I'll show you around."

"Okay." But Georgie didn't sit down. Instead she walked over to the opposite wall where several black-and-white framed photographs were hung. She studied them with interest. The first showed a familiar actor shaking hands with Bill Clinton. She idly wondered why a photo of Patrick Dempsey would be hanging in the foundation's office. Had he made a big contribution or been involved in a recent humanitarian effort on behalf of the foundation? He and the former president were the only ones she recognized. The other photos were of people she didn't know, people who were obviously either supporters or workers for the foundation. She only glanced at them, thinking it was likely one of the men in those photos was her new boss, Zachary Prince.

"Miss Fairchild?"

Georgie whipped around. She hadn't heard Deborah's return.

"Our one claim to fame," Deborah said, walking over and pointing to the photo of the actor and Bill Clinton.

"What did Patrick Dempsey do for the foundation?" Georgie asked.

Deborah rolled her eyes. "Oh, boy. Zach *hates* that."

"Hates what?"

"When people think he's Patrick Dempsey. He gets it all the time. Women have been known to follow him on the street. One or two have even followed him to the office. And let's not even talk about the paparazzi." She shook her head. "They've been fooled by the resemblance, too."

Georgie stared at Deborah. "That's Zachary Prince? Not Patrick Dempsey?"

"Yep. That's Zach."

Geez Louise. Georgie didn't trust gorgeous men. In fact, aside from Alex, she'd never met one who wasn't full of himself. *I knew I wasn't going to like this assignment, and that conviction just got a lot stronger.*

Deborah was still chuckling as she said, "C'mon, I'll give you the ten-cent tour now."

It didn't take long to see the rest of the offices. There were only three of them, plus a small conference room, a tiny kitchen and a unisex bathroom. The largest office was Zachary Prince's, Deborah explained. Georgie only caught a glimpse of it, because they didn't go inside. The office assigned to Georgie was directly across the hall, and next door to hers was an office that was used by everyone and anyone associated with the foundation at any given time.

"Including visitors and temporary help," Deborah said. "We pretty much operate on a shoestring. Zach doesn't believe in wasting money that can be used in better places."

Good, Georgie thought. At least he and she would agree in one area. "Where is Mr. Prince?"

Deborah smiled. "Oh, don't call him Mr. Prince. He'd hate that, too. He's Zach to everyone."

Georgie noticed that Deborah hadn't answered her question. She was just about to pose it again, when Deborah said, "To answer your question, Zach doesn't usually get here before ten."

Oh, really? Strike two, Georgie thought, only barely preventing herself from rolling her eyes the way Deborah had earlier. Georgie could just imagine why he couldn't make it in early. She'd known a few of his type—pretty boys who did the club scene at night. No wonder Alex was concerned about the New York office, even if he hadn't seen fit to tell her exactly why he was concerned.

She was still thinking about the things Deborah had told her, even as she unpacked her satchel and arranged the supplies piled upon her desk. She hoped she was wrong. She hoped Zach Prince would turn out to be just as great as Alex had made him out to be. But she had a bad feeling that Alex had kept things from her.

And even if he hadn't, even if he really thought Zachary Prince was terrific, there was always a first time to be fooled, especially when you were operating long distance from each other. In fact, maybe the reason they so desperately needed to hire an assistant here was because the assistant actually did all the work. And who knew?

Maybe down deep, Alex suspected as much, even if he wouldn't, or couldn't, put his suspicions into words.

Georgie had just finished setting everything up to her liking, booting up her company-issue laptop and logging on to the employee section of the foundation's website, where she'd begun reading the reports of weekend activity posted by various field agents and other foundation employees, when she heard a male voice talking to Deborah, then the footsteps of someone coming down the hall.

Mr. Gorgeous had finally arrived, she guessed.

Sure enough, a few seconds later, the Patrick Dempsey lookalike stood in her open doorway. "Good morning," he said.

Bad night, she thought, eyeing his rumpled, longish black hair and tired eyes. Probably out way too late. "Good morning."

"Zach Prince," he said, walking in. He wore a dark business suit under a black topcoat.

Georgie stood. "Georgie Fairchild." They shook hands. His handshake was firm but not crushing, a minor point in his favor. Georgie hated when men tried to show you how strong they were with a handshake from hell.

He looked at her desk. "Sorry I wasn't here earlier, but I see Deborah has taken care of you."

"Yes, she has."

"Give me a half hour or so to get some things organized, then we'll talk."

If Georgie had been him, she'd have been here an hour before the new person was scheduled to arrive. She'd have been ready to talk immediately. "All right," she agreed.

Not a good beginning, she thought as she watched

him walk across the hall and into his office. When he shut the door behind him, she shook her head. *Not a good beginning at all.*

Hell, Zach thought. He could see, just from the way she looked at him, that Georgie Fairchild was judging him and finding him wanting. He could easily imagine what she thought. Not only was he later than usual—10:30 by his watch—but he probably looked like he'd been out all night. Added to that was the way he looked, which caused people who didn't know him to think he was a lightweight.

One look at Georgie Fairchild and anyone could see that *she* wasn't a lightweight. Her height alone—Zach guessed she was about five ten or eleven—would be intimidating to a lot of people. It wasn't to Zach—he was well over six feet himself—but he would imagine it gave her an advantage in a lot of situations.

In addition to her height were businesslike clothes, a utilitarian watch, no jewelry except tiny diamond earrings, thick wheat-blond hair pulled back into a no-nonsense ponytail, cool green eyes, subtle makeup—it was obvious to anyone that here was a young woman who was capable, efficient and self-confident.

Zach groaned inwardly. All his reservations about Georgie Fairchild bubbled up. He'd been right to be concerned. Having her here was not a good idea. Zach felt like picking up the phone and calling Alex right now and saying, "No way, José." So what if she had an honorary seat on the HuntCom board?

In fact, if she gave him one bit of trouble, she was going to be out of here. But if worse came to worst, if Alex really *had* sent her here for some ulterior motive, then Zach's ongoing work-versus home dilemma might solve itself.

Feeling better now that he'd decided on his modus operandi, he booted up his laptop and opened his email account.

It was almost 11:30 before Zach—she couldn't keep referring to him as Zachary Prince, even in her own mind—called Georgie into his office. She kept telling herself to keep an open mind, but if she was being honest with herself, she'd admit she'd pretty much formed her opinion of him already. Maybe he was as good as Alex had said he was, but his work habits told another story.

He stood as she walked into the office. Okay, so he'd been taught nice manners and they extended into the workplace, but as far as Georgie was concerned, standing for her was another strike against him, because all the gesture meant was that he thought of her more as a woman than a colleague.

"I understand you got here on Friday," he said as they both took a seat—him behind the desk, her in one of the two chairs flanking it. There was also a long leather sofa along the side wall and several framed watercolors hanging above it.

"Yes."

He must have noticed her looking at the watercolors, because he said, "My sister painted those."

"They're lovely." And they were. Georgie would have liked to look at them more closely.

"Thank you," he said, still in that rather formal voice. "So, have you been to the city before?"

"No, this is my first time."

"What do you think of it?"

"So far, I like it."

"How's the apartment?"

"It's very nice, thank you." Georgie hesitated, then added, "I appreciate that you stocked the pantry and refrigerator for me."

"That was Deborah's doing."

"I'll have to thank her, then."

For a few minutes, they talked about the sights she'd taken in over the weekend, and just as Georgie was beginning to think he'd never get down to business, he said, "Shall we get started?"

I thought you'd never ask. "I'm ready anytime you are."

He picked up a large blue bound notebook, and as he did so, Georgie noticed the two framed photos on his desk, which the notebook had partially hidden. Without staring, she could see that one was a photo of three children—one of whom looked quite young—and the other was of a very pretty dark-haired woman.

So maybe he wasn't a playboy type? Of course, the kids could be nieces and nephews. The woman could be the sister he'd mentioned, but she couldn't imagine any man keeping his sister's framed picture on his desk.

Even though she'd thought she wasn't obviously looking, she must have been, because he said, "My family."

Georgie's eyes met his. "Nice looking."

"Thank you."

He looked away, but not before she caught a glimpse of some emotion in his eyes she didn't quite understand. It almost looked like sadness. Surely not. But as quickly as it had appeared, the emotion, whatever it was, had disappeared.

For the next hour they pored over the various grants

the eastern division of the foundation had pledged in the past quarter and the projects they were in the process of considering, plus a list of possible beneficiaries that had had preliminary vetting but which needed in-depth research and investigation. Zach also handed her a stack of grant applications that hadn't been vetted at all. "We call these our slush pile," he said.

As Zach talked, giving her background material and status reports, Georgie had to admit he seemed to know his business. He answered all her questions thoroughly and only once had to refer to another source to give her the information she requested. After a while, he seemed to warm up to her, and once or twice he actually smiled.

Good heavens, that smile should be banned, she thought as she found herself responding to its warmth... and potent sexiness. This last thought alarmed her so much she actually backed up in her chair. The last thing she wanted—or needed—was to feel any attraction, even the tiniest bit, for Zachary Prince. She kept her expression as businesslike and cool as she could manage while reminding herself he was a) so not her type, b) her boss, and c), most importantly, married.

She tried to banish her disturbing thoughts with limited success. Finally they finished with the blue book, which Zach had told her they called their bible, and he said, "Since it's already one o'clock, why don't you take a lunch break? In the meantime, I'll ask Deborah to pull all the active files for you to study this afternoon. I'd like you to pay particular attention to the Carlyle Children's Cancer Center because that's the first possible beneficiary I want you to do a final evaluation on."

"All right." She couldn't wait to get back to her office. And away from him.

"If you have questions, make a note of them. We can discuss them tomorrow morning." Then he added, "I won't be here this afternoon." His blue eyes met hers squarely. This time he didn't smile. Nor did he offer any explanation.

Georgie told herself he was the boss and he had a perfect right to come and go as he pleased. And he certainly didn't have to justify himself to her, did he? Besides, he could have perfectly legitimate business to take care of. She told herself where he might be going or what he might be doing wasn't her concern and she shouldn't jump to any conclusions. She told herself she was there to do a job, that Alex had not asked her to report back about Zach *or* his work habits and no matter how she felt about Zach herself, she was going to do that job to the best of her ability. And she was going to keep her relationship with Zach strictly business. In fact, the less she knew about him and the less she saw of him, the better off she'd be. She might not have been here long, but she already knew Zachary Prince was bad news—on more than one level.

As Georgie returned to her office, she couldn't help thinking how right she'd been to resist coming to New York.

Chapter Four

"I'm glad you could come in this afternoon, Mr. Prince. I know you're a busy man."

Zach liked the counselor at his children's private school. Celeste Fouchet had proven herself to be compassionate and intelligent, and she had a great rapport with the students. Katie liked her; he knew she did, even though his daughter didn't talk about her counseling sessions at home.

"Nothing is more important than my children," he said, taking the seat the counselor had indicated.

"I noticed that Katie is out sick today," Miss Fouchet said.

"Yes. She's got a strep infection. Dr. Noble saw her this morning and said we'd need to keep her home until she's no longer contagious."

"Well, I hope she feels better soon." The counselor smiled. "The reason I asked you to come and see me is

I'm still a bit worried about Katie." Unlike some others who might have avoided his eyes or fiddled with something on her desk, she met his gaze directly.

In her gray eyes, he saw sympathy. His heart sank. He'd hoped the summons from the counselor had meant that Katie didn't need additional help, that she'd finally accepted her mother's death.

"I thought she was doing really well," he said. "I haven't heard her crying at night in a long time."

Miss Fouchet nodded. "She is doing better, but she's still not where I'd like her to be. She's accepted her mother's death, and she also knows no one is to blame, that it was the disease that took your wife, not anything she or anyone else did wrong. That's a good thing, because for a long time she was secretly blaming herself."

"Which was totally irrational."

"Yes, but we all think irrational thoughts when we're devastated by loss. Very few of us have objectivity in times of great pain."

Zach sighed. "I know." God knows that for a while he'd blamed himself, too. Why had he not seen Jenny's symptoms so that he could have insisted she see a doctor sooner? *If only he'd done this…or that…* He grimaced. *If only.* Those two words were the most useless words in the dictionary. "What else can I do to help Katie?"

"Just keep doing what you're doing: loving her and reassuring her anytime she begins to show signs of her fear of losing you, too." The counselor gave him an understanding smile. "I know it's hard. I know you want to make every bad thing go away for Katie, but healing from a loss like this is a slow process, Mr. Prince. It doesn't happen overnight."

"I know, but it has been two years." Jeremy had

seemed to snap back to his old self within months of Jenny's death. Then again, he was only four when Jenny first got sick. He'd quickly adapted to the fact that his mother couldn't do the things she'd always done, so her loss hadn't affected him in the same way it had affected Katie. *And me.*

"Each of us is different. Some of us deal with these things better than others. In your case, you're stronger than Katie…and wiser. For a girl, losing a mother is traumatic. And for a girl Katie's age—on the cusp of her teen years—it's life-changing. But your daughter is going to be all right, I feel quite sure of that. I just wanted you to know that we're not there yet. And I wanted to tell you again now much I like your daughter." Her expression softened. "Katie's a special girl. She's going to be a remarkable woman someday."

Zach suddenly found it hard to speak around the lump in his throat. "She's…very like her mother."

The warmth in the counselor's eyes said she understood exactly how he was feeling. "I suspected as much. She talks about her mother with so much…love and gentleness."

Zach managed to get a grip on his emotions, but once he stepped outside and began the twenty-block walk home—he'd decided he could use the exercise today—that feeling of emptiness and loss returned with a strength he hadn't felt in months. And he knew— sadly—that both he and his oldest daughter, at least, still had a ways to go before they'd be completely whole again.

"So how was your first day at work?"

Georgie made a face. "It was fine."

"Georgie, I can tell just by the tone of your voice that it wasn't fine," Joanna said.

So Georgie, who hadn't planned to say a word until Joanna had called and begun pumping her, spilled the whole story—how Zach Prince had showed up at the office so late, how he'd skipped out again without any explanation about where he might be going, how she felt even more uneasy about him now than she'd felt before—and then she even found herself telling Joanna how good-looking he was.

"Really?" Joanna said. "He actually looks like Patrick Dempsey? Gee, he can't be *that* hard to work with, then. At least you've got something great to look at! I mean, he didn't act obnoxious or anything, did he?"

"No."

"Well, then? How bad can it be? Just sit back and enjoy the scenery for a while."

Joanna's comments caused Georgie to remember what she'd said to her sisters a while back when they'd started bugging her about getting married. "What?" Bobbie had said. "You're going to go without sex for the rest of your life?" And Georgie had laughed and retaliated, saying she hadn't said a thing about going without sex, that she intended to have plenty of lovers.

Now why on earth had Joanna's comment about Zach made her think of *that* conversation?

"Speaking of scenery," Georgie said, "how's your romance going?"

"Chick's wonderful," Joanna said dreamily. "Oh, Georgie, you should try it."

"Try what?" But Georgie knew.

"Being in love. There's no feeling like it in the world."

Later that night, as Georgie slathered moisturizer on

her face in preparation for bed, she thought about her conversation with Joanna again. She was glad she hadn't confessed the momentary attraction she'd felt toward Zach, especially since soon after that she'd discovered he was married. Georgie knew it wasn't uncommon to be attracted to people who were out of bounds. Shoot, she wouldn't be human if she could turn off physical reactions the way you turned off a TV remote. Still, the memory of her involuntary physical response to Zach's smile continued to plague her even after she'd climbed into bed and turned off the bedside lamp, because it had been such a strong response, the likes of which she hadn't had in a long time.

Her last thought before drifting off to sleep was that tomorrow she would redouble her efforts to be a perfectly controlled, perfectly businesslike employee. And hopefully, her future assignments would keep her well away from the office...and from Zachary Prince and his damned smile.

"You look beautiful, as always, Corny."

Cornelia kept her voice light as she answered, although the expression in Harry's dark eyes unleashed some unwanted butterflies. "Always the flatterer, aren't you, Harry?"

He smiled. "I mean every word. No one would ever believe you're sixty-six. Why, today you don't look a day over forty."

"Oh, please," Cornelia scoffed. "Don't exaggerate. Fifty maybe. But forty?"

"You're more beautiful now than you were as a young girl," he insisted.

The two of them were having a late lunch at a charming lodge-type restaurant out near the Hunt mansion. It was a typical Seattle winter day—cold and gloomy and threatening rain at any moment—but the lodge had a cheery fire going in their big stone fireplace, and Harry had secured a table close by the inviting warmth. And, of course, Cornelia had ridden to their lunch date in comfort and style, because Harry had sent Walter, his long-time driver, to pick her up in the Lincoln Town Car.

"You don't look so bad yourself," she said with a chuckle. "For a seventy-two-year-old man, that is." Harry was still as tall as he'd been as a young man—topping six feet four—with the hawklike features and thick hair that had always been the standard by which Cornelia measured other men.

He laughed. "You just couldn't resist letting me know that I'm an old geezer, could you?"

"You know I was teasing you."

His smile faded, and he reached across the table to take her hand. "Were you? Maybe you really do think I'm too old."

Cornelia's wayward heart betrayed her at the look in his eyes. What was happening here? she wondered. She was afraid to hope. For so long, she'd hoped to no avail. She couldn't go through that again. She'd been disappointed too many times. "Too old for what, Harry?" she said carefully.

"Too old to try again."

"To try *what* again?" Cornelia wasn't going to make anything easy for him. Not after what he'd put her through.

"You're going to make me beg, aren't you?"

Cornelia refused to look away. Instead, she met his gaze squarely. Almost defiantly.

"Beg for what, Harry?"

"For you, Corny. For you. I let you slip through my fingers once. And that was a big mistake. Maybe the biggest I've ever made."

"Yes, you did."

"Well? What do you think?"

"What do *you* think, Harry?"

"I think we belong together."

"I once thought we did, too. But you couldn't wait for me to grow up, could you? Instead, you picked all those other women." For the first time, she couldn't hide from him the bitterness she thought she'd eradicated.

"Hell, Corny, I know I was stupid. I'm trying to tell you that. I guess my pride was hurt." He shrugged. "I was young, too. I may have been smart when it came to electronics and computers, but I didn't have much experience with life. Certainly not with women." His dark gaze shined intently as he put more pressure on her hand. "Cornelia, I love you. I always have loved you. And I don't want us to waste another minute. I want us to be together for as many years as we've got left."

Cornelia's traitorous heart was now pounding. But she was determined not to make this easy for him. He'd hurt her too much in the past. He needed to suffer a bit, too! *There are none so blind as those who will not see.* The familiar line from the Bible stiffened her resolve as she reminded herself of all the years of Harry's cluelessness. If he really had come to his senses and wanted her now, he was going to have to work for her. "I might want that, too," she said, "but right now, I'm not sure. I need some time."

His gaze narrowed. "Is it that golf pro? Dammit, Corny, he's too young for you."

Cornelia yanked her hand away. "Is that so? Well, maybe I don't agree." She had half a mind to get up and walk out on him, even though their dessert hadn't yet been served. She knew Walter would take her home. He liked her better than Harry, anyway. And how did Harry know about Greg?

"Ah, come on, Corny, stop it. You know we belong together." Harry reached into his inside jacket pocket and took out a small black velvet box. Snapping it open, he showed her the ring inside. "I bought this for you. I want you to marry me."

Cornelia almost gasped, but she stopped herself just in time. Sitting there was one of the most magnificent rings she'd ever set eyes on. A huge round pink diamond circled by dozens of tiny diamonds, it was set in what she figured was platinum—nothing but the best for Harrison Hunt—and it was breathtaking. The ring would probably overpower her slender hand, but that was Harry. He did nothing by small measures. Gathering every ounce of strength she possessed, she said quietly, "That's quite a ring, Harry."

"Is that all you have to say? I said I was sorry, Corny. I said I was stupid. I said loved you. I said I wanted us to spend the rest of our lives together. What more can I say?"

"Oh, I think you can say a lot more, Harry. And if you're really serious, if you really mean everything you've said tonight, then you'll be quite willing to court me the way you should."

"The way I *should?*"

"Don't sound so incredulous or I may decide I'm not interested no matter what you do…or say."

For a long moment, he just looked at her. She knew she'd shocked him. She knew he'd expected her to fall at his feet. After all, very few people, and *no women* that she knew of, had ever said no to him. Harry Hunt had always been able to buy anything he wanted. Well, she wasn't for sale. And the sooner he knew that, the better.

Finally he sighed. "You win, Corny. You want me to court you, I will. You want me to grovel, I will." His smile this time was almost humble. Almost. "Because I really do love you, Corny, with all my heart. And I'll prove it to you. We *are* going to spend the rest of our lives together, and that's a promise."

For Georgie, at least, Day Two at the office began earlier than Day One. Deborah had given Georgie a key, so she decided she didn't have to wait till nine to get a start on her workday. Always a morning person, she was at her desk before eight and reading all the information she could find on the Carlyle Children's Cancer Center. She was almost finished with a preliminary report on her findings when she heard Zach arrive. A glance at her watch showed it was a few minutes before ten. She stood, hoping she could talk to him before he got involved in anything else.

But except for a quick "Good morning," and "It'll have to wait," in answer to her query about a meeting, he spent the remaining hours before lunch closeted in his office, where she could faintly hear him talking on the phone.

What was so important that he couldn't at least answer a few questions? The longer his door remained shut, the more irritated she became. What did he expect her to do? Sit and twiddle her thumbs until he was ready to pay some attention to her? She'd already read everything she could find about every single funded and non-funded agency they currently worked with or were considering. The only thing she hadn't yet attacked was the "slush pile." She eyed it thoughtfully. She didn't want to muddy the waters by reading through all those applications before she and Zach had had a chance to talk in more depth about the ones already in process.

Huffing out a frustrated sigh, she wished she were the kind of person who could pick up the phone, call Alex and tell him exactly what she thought about Prince Zach, the pretty boy with the questionable work habits. Finally, when her watch read 12:30 and her stomach started telling her it needed food, she decided she might as well go to lunch.

She debated knocking on Zach's door to tell him she was leaving, then changed her mind. *The hell with him. If he wants me, he can just wait till I get back.*

She told Deborah she was going to get something to eat, then walked to a small deli a few doors away from her building. Forty minutes later, revived by tuna salad, cheese and fruit, she returned to the office and found that Zach was indeed waiting for her. In fact, he was sitting on the corner of Deborah's desk and stood when she opened the door.

"I read your report on the Carlyle Center," he said. "I thought we could visit there this afternoon. I want to introduce you to the principals, and I think it'll be helpful to hear in person their arguments for the grant they've applied for."

"I'd like that, but in the future, if you think we'll be visiting one of our prospective grant recipients, I wish you'd let me know the day before." Georgie knew she sounded stiff, but dammit, if she'd known they'd be calling on the Carlyle people, she'd have worn something a bit more professional. She made a mental note to make sure to keep a suit and heels at the office so she wouldn't be blindsided in the future.

"Oh?" Zach seemed taken aback by her tone. "What's the problem?"

"The problem is, I don't feel dressed appropriately." Today she'd worn russet wool slacks and a matching cowl-necked sweater. And flat shoes.

Zach's gaze swept over her. "You look perfectly fine. We're not going to some fashion house. It's a hospital."

"I realize that." Men simply didn't get it when it came to clothes. They always wore the same thing. Maybe that's what she should do, too. Wear a suit every day and only vary the color of her blouse. But even though Georgie pretended she didn't care about clothes or fashion, the truth was, she liked to look good. And she also liked the feeling of control wearing a professional outfit always gave her.

"You look fine," he said again.

Georgie would have liked to say something else, but she knew if she did, she would just sound petulant. Worse, she'd sound like a silly woman. So she swallowed the smart remark and simply shrugged.

Zach, unfortunately, looked better than he had yesterday, mainly because the dark circles were gone from his eyes, and he'd obviously made an effort to tame his unruly hair. Why was it men could do the minimum in grooming and manage to look great?

"Oh, all right," she said. "Just give me a minute, okay?" She wanted to at least brush her teeth first. Because a person's smile was the first thing *she* noticed, Georgie was a fanatic when it came to her teeth—brushing after every meal, flossing nightly and making periodic visits to the dentist—usually between every assignment in the field.

Five minutes later, teeth clean and makeup freshened, she joined Zach, who again waited in the outer office.

"It's a good two miles," he said when they walked out of their building. "I'll get us a cab."

"I don't mind walking," Georgie said. "It'll be good exercise."

"The streets are messy, and I don't want to be splattered with dirty snow when we get there."

Georgie hated that she agreed with him. "Okay, fine."

A typical New Yorker, Zach stepped right out into the street and stuck his arm out. Within minutes, a cab pulled up. Georgie had already figured out that when the center dome light was on, a cab was free.

When Zach climbed into the back first, Georgie was surprised. But she quickly realized that he was the one who had to slide over to the other side and that it was much easier then for her to get in. "Thanks," she said.

"For what?" He leaned forward and gave the driver the address of the cancer center.

"For not making me slide over to where you're sitting."

There was that smile of his again. And dammit, it produced the same effect it had produced the day before. What was *wrong* with her? She didn't even *like* him.

"I learned about that kind of thing a long time ago," he said, still smiling. "I have a twin sister, and she educated me about women and skirts and heels." He chuckled. "Among other things."

"But I don't have a skirt on," Georgie retorted, just to be perverse.

The smile remained. In fact, now his eyes twinkled. "But you *are* a woman."

And just the way he said it, Georgie knew he thought

she was attractive, and her face heated. Thank God the cab's interior was shaded. Oh, she hated her tendency to blush. She decided the best thing she could do was ignore the remark. "So you're a twin," she said instead.

"Yep."

"Any brothers?"

"Nope. Just Sabrina. What about you?"

"I have three sisters." She was surprised he didn't know that. After all, all four Fairchilds had honorary seats on the HuntCom board.

"Younger? Older?" he asked.

"All younger." Georgie didn't intend to say more. More than ever, considering her unwanted reaction to him, she intended to keep their relationship strictly business. But he seemed so genuinely interested, she added, "But we're stair-steps. Only one year between each of us."

"Any brothers?"

"Unfortunately, no. And my dad wanted a boy desperately. That's why we have the names we do." Forgetting she didn't like him and hadn't intended to be friendly, she laughed and said, "My dad's name was George."

Zach laughed, too. "What about your sisters? Do they all have boys' names, too?"

"Afraid so. Frankie—actually, Francesca—is named for my dad's brother. Bobbie was going to be Robert, and Tommi would have been Thomas." Georgie made a face. "When we were younger, we all hated our names. There I was, in class with a million Heathers and Tiffanys and Kims…and me with a name like Georgie. And, of course, being the tallest girl in my class didn't help."

"My sister's tall, too. She also hated it when she was young, but now she realizes it's an advantage."

Just then the driver asked a question, and after Zach had answered, he said he wanted to give her a brief rundown on the two main contacts she would be working with at Carlyle during her evaluation of the cancer center. "Jonathan Pierce can be hard to deal with," he began.

Georgie had familiarized herself with Dr. Pierce's background that morning. A specialist, Pierce had sixteen years' experience in pediatric oncology/hematology, had trained at Memorial Sloan Kettering Cancer Center and was board certified in both specialties.

"Why is he hard to deal with?"

"He's a sought-after doctor who is highly regarded, but he resents the fact that the foundation required the center to meet certain conditions to be eligible for one of our grants."

"But that's standard practice with nonprofits, isn't it?"

"Yes," Zach said. "Yet I can understand how he feels. Pierce is passionate about what they do at Carlyle. He expected to be approved immediately. Whereas Carolyn Love, the CFO—she's the other one you'll meet today—is more tolerant of our position, because she understands budgetary constraints and that we have a board to answer to."

Just then, the cab pulled up to the entrance of the center, which was a division of Carlyle Clinic, and a few minutes later they were on their way to the third floor, where the administrative offices were located.

"I think it would be best if you let me do the talking today," Zach said as they stepped off the elevator.

Georgie bristled. "Why?"

"Because, as I said before, Pierce can be a tough nut."

"So? I'll have to deal with him sometime."

"I know, but it'll be better if we ease him into the new relationship."

"You don't trust me, do you?"

"It's not that I don't trust you, it's that I'm used to Pierce. You're not."

"Seems to me letting me take charge today would be the best way to get used to him."

"Look, bottom line? He can be a bit arrogant when it comes to women."

Oh, great. Fortunately, most of the men Georgie'd worked with during her time with the Hunt Foundation were the opposite; most didn't care what your gender was, they were simply grateful for any help they could get. Of course, that didn't always hold true for some of the bureaucrats she'd had dealings with. She'd often wondered why the least important political hack put on the most airs. The way she'd always dealt with these types was to let them know right off the bat that she wasn't going to put up with any B.S. from them…or anyone.

"Look," she said to Zach, "I am not one of those seen-but-not-heard women. And I refuse to pretend to be."

Zach sighed. "I can't stop you from talking. But it would make things a lot easier for everyone if you'd just back off a little. You and I know you're going to be in charge, and Jonathan Pierce will soon know it, too. I just don't want to rub his nose in it today, okay?"

"Oh, all right," she finally said. "I'll keep my mouth shut and let you do the talking." *This time.*

Maybe the expression on her face gave away her thoughts, because he raised his eyebrows. "Why do I get the feeling Jonathan Pierce better watch out?"

Chapter Five

The meeting hadn't been too bad, Georgie thought. Although Zach had done most of the talking, she hadn't felt like a fifth wheel, because he'd included her in his remarks, saying things like, "I know Miss Fairchild agrees," or "After today, please contact Miss Fairchild with any questions or concerns."

She'd only broken her promise to Zach once, and that was at the very end of their meeting, when they'd all stood and were saying their goodbyes. Georgie had turned to Carolyn Love—and Zach had been right about her: She was businesslike, and Georgie immediately liked her—to say she'd call for an appointment in the next few days, and Jonathan Pierce had said, pointedly, to Zach, "Call me as soon as you've made your decision, Zach, so I can get that new equipment ordered."

Before Zach could open his mouth to reply, Georgie said, also pointedly, "Dr. Pierce, you've already been told that it's me you'll be dealing with from now on. I'll be the one calling you."

Pierce's gray eyes had darkened, and he'd glared at her. But before he could reply, Zach said, "Yes, Jonathan, Miss Fairchild will be contacting you."

They were saved additional histrionics by the doctor's pager going off, and he'd abruptly left the small conference room where the meeting had taken place, but not before giving Georgie the evil eye. She almost laughed. Her eyes had met Zach's and he'd winked.

Maybe I've misjudged him, she thought grudgingly.

She and Zach rode the elevator down to the main floor in silence. There were hospital personnel getting on and off; it paid to be discreet.

Georgie tightened her scarf as they exited the building. She was also glad she was wearing warm leather gloves, because the temperature seemed to have dropped while they were inside. Or maybe the contrast between the warm building and the bitterly cold February wind just made it feel colder out. Georgie did notice how quickly most of the people on the sidewalk were moving, most with their heads down.

Before hailing a cab, Zach turned to her and said, "Do you mind if we stop off at my apartment before going back to the office? I left some files there that I meant to bring with me this morning."

"No, that's fine."

A cab pulled over almost immediately, and they got in. Georgie found she was actually looking forward to seeing where Zach lived. Maybe she'd even get to meet his wife.

"My oldest daughter is home sick today," he said after giving the driver their destination. "She's got a strep infection."

"I used to get those when I was a kid. They're not any fun."

"No. She was pretty miserable yesterday, but the antibiotic seems to be doing its job. She seemed better this morning."

Georgie knew it was none of her business, but he'd given her an opening, so she said, "Is that why you left the office early yesterday afternoon?"

He only hesitated a moment before shaking his head. "No. I had an appointment at Katie's school." He sighed. "She's had a rough time since her mother died."

Georgie's mouth went dry. "Your...your wife *died?*"

"Yes. Jenny...had cancer."

"I'm so sorry."

"Thank you."

Georgie's mind spun. A lot of her ideas about Zach had been wrong, then. He wasn't married. And he wasn't a playboy who stayed out late every night. He was a widower with three young children. *That'll teach me to be so judgmental, to jump to conclusions about people.*

What else had she been wrong about? Maybe he wasn't a slacker as far as work was concerned, either. He certainly had conducted himself well today, and he definitely seemed to know what he was talking about. She could see that both Jonathan Pierce and Carolyn Love respected him. And Love, in particular, had impressed Georgie as the kind of businesswoman who wouldn't be easy to fool.

Georgie wondered if Zach would say anything more, but he turned away from her and stared out the window on his side...or pretended to. She wondered how long ago his wife had died. Maybe his children weren't as young as she'd originally thought. Maybe that photo on his desk had been taken a while ago. But she'd be willing to bet that Zach was only in his thirties. He certainly didn't look any older than that. So unless he'd married right out of high school, which she was certain wouldn't be the case, his children couldn't be that old.

Now she was avidly curious about him. Why hadn't Alex informed her that Zach was a widower? Yet why should he? She realized Alex rarely repeated anything personal about any of the Hunt Foundation employees, especially since she'd begun working for him. Actually, she appreciated his respect for their privacy. That told her he would not have discussed anything personal about her, either, not with Zach and not with any of the people she'd worked with or for.

Her mind teemed with unanswered questions during the ten-minute cab ride. When the taxi pulled up in front of an apartment building on W. 66th Street, right around the corner from Lincoln Center, Georgie blinked in surprise. Even as a newcomer to the city, she recognized that they were in a high-rent district.

As they exited the cab, a uniformed doorman opened the door of the building as soon as he recognized Zach, saying, "Good afternoon, Mr. Prince."

"Good afternoon, Thomas."

The doorman smiled at Georgie.

There was a security guard sitting at a desk in the lobby of the building, and he, too, called Zach by name. "Cold one out there today," he said as they approached.

"Sure is," Zach said, then added, "How's Mona doing?"

"Better," the guard said. "She'll get her cast off next week."

"I know she'll be glad." Turning to Georgie, Zach

said, "This way," and led her around the corner to a bank of three elevators.

Georgie couldn't help thinking what a fortune this building must cost to live in. How did Zach afford it? She knew his job at the foundation couldn't begin to pay enough to live on this scale. In fact, she knew, because Alex had recently mentioned it, that the board of directors had been talking about raises for the administrative staff since salaries at the Hunt Foundation had been found to be lower than comparable companies, and if they wanted to remain competitive and attract the best employees, they had to spend some money.

When the elevator doors opened on the eleventh floor, Georgie wouldn't have been at all surprised to find they were already in Zach's apartment, but instead they walked out into a hallway. There were two entrances that Georgie could see. Zach headed for a double doorway midway down the right side of the hall. After unlocking the doors, he gestured her ahead of him.

They entered a small foyer containing an antique lowboy upon which sat an ornate Chinese vase filled with fresh flowers. "It's me, Fanny," Zach called. Seconds later, an attractive fifty-something woman with dark hair and a pleasant smile greeted them.

"Fanny, this is Georgie Fairchild, my new assistant. Georgie, I'd like you to meet Fanny Whittaker, our housekeeper and the one person I can't live without."

Georgie smiled and shook the woman's hand. The housekeeper's hazel eyes, filled with intelligence, gave Georgie a quick once-over.

"How's Katie doing?" Zach asked.

"She's much better today, Mr. Prince. In fact, she's watching a movie now. I fixed her some tea and cinnamon toast."

"And where's Emma?" He turned to Georgie. "Emma's my three-year-old. Normally, when she's around, you can't get a word in edgewise."

"Sabrina took her for the day," Fanny said.

"Sabrina's a saint."

"Well, Emma was driving poor Katie crazy. She wanted to play Go Fish and wouldn't take no for an answer."

Zach shook his head. "She's a pistol," he said to Georgie. "When she sets her mind to something, you cannot sway her."

Georgie laughed. "Sounds like me when I was little. Actually, my sisters would say that sounds like me *now*."

"Uh-oh," Zach said. "That doesn't bode well for me, does it?"

Georgie shrugged. "We'll see. Depends on whether you agree with me or not."

Now it was his turn to laugh. "C'mon, I'll introduce you to Katie."

A few minutes later, they stood in the family room, whose windows faced Central Park. Although it was bitterly cold outside, the afternoon sun gave the illusion of warmth as it streamed through the windows. Katie was propped against pillows on one of two matching love seats and covered by a gaily patterned quilt. A TV tray sat next to her, and Georgie could see the remnants of her snack along with a box of tissues.

Zach's daughter had his dark hair, but her eyes were a warm brown and her face was heart-shaped. Even seated, Georgie could tell she was petite. Her face lit up at her father's appearance. "Hi, Dad."

"Hi, honey. Fanny tells me you're feeling better today."

Katie nodded. "Lots better."

"Katie, I want you to meet my new assistant. This is Miss Fairchild. Georgie, this is my daughter Katie."

"Hi, Katie."

"Hello, Miss Fairchild."

"Oh, please. Call me Georgie. Everyone does." Georgie smiled at the girl.

Katie studied her as if considering. Her expression remained noncommital.

"We had a meeting at the Carlyle Clinic and we're on our way back to the office," Zach said. "We just stopped by to pick up some files."

"Oh."

There was no mistaking the disappointment in Katie's voice.

"I'm sorry, honey. I'll try to be home early. In the meantime, get a lot of rest. When I get home, we'll have a game of chess."

She gave him a dubious look. "Emma and Jeremy will be here by then."

"I know, but we'll still have our game, I promise."

Katie shrugged. "Whatever." In that gesture, Georgie saw all the times Katie's interests had had to take a backseat to her younger siblings' demands for attention. Georgie could relate. As much as she now loved her sisters, she could remember all those times she wished they'd just disappear.

Bending down, Zach kissed his daughter on the cheek. "We've got to get back to the office now, but I'll be home no later than six."

Katie sighed. "Okay." She picked up the remote and before they'd even left the room, Georgie saw that the movie was playing again.

* * *

Cornelia hated being late. She felt it was rude and sent the message that you thought your time was more valuable than the person's you were meeting. But today her lateness was unavoidable, because when she'd gotten in her car she'd discovered her battery was dead.

She'd immediately called Kit Hoover, the old friend she was meeting for lunch at the club, and Kit said not to worry. Then Cornelia had called a cab. She simply didn't have time to deal with her car this morning.

"You're looking very chic today," Kit said as Cornelia approached their table, where Kit was already halfway through a glass of wine. She eyed Cornelia over the tops of her oversized red frames, which she wore perched halfway down her nose. Kit kept her short hair dyed the black of her youth and had half a dozen pairs of glasses with bright frames that matched her outfits. Today was no exception; she wore a fire-engine-red pants suit.

"Thank you. So are you. I like the red," Cornelia said, sitting opposite her friend. Cornelia rarely, if ever, wore primary colors, favoring instead the soft, muted shades that were more suitable to her peaches-and-cream coloring.

"And I love that sea-green dress," Kit said. "On you, at any rate." She drank another healthy slug of wine.

Cornelia told herself she was not Kit's mother, nor was it her job to monitor how much Kit drank. But sometimes Kit's tendency to over-imbibe bothered Cornelia.

They didn't talk while Cornelia looked over the menu, then gave their orders to their waiter, an older man who had been working at the club almost as long as Cornelia had been a member. He greeted Cornelia with a big smile. "Nice to see you again, Ms. Fairchild," he said.

"Thank you, Fred."

After he left to place their orders, Kit said, "So what's new? I feel like I haven't seen you in weeks."

"That's because you haven't," Cornelia said, laughing. "Well, let's see. My Seattle-based girls are all busy and happily in love."

"What about Georgie? She still roaming around the world?"

Cornelia was in the middle of telling Kit about Georgie's new job in New York when Kit suddenly sat up straighter, looked beyond Cornelia and said, "Well, hello, Greg."

Cornelia's heart gave a little hop, and she turned around. She hadn't seen the golf pro for a while; he'd been participating in a tournament in Hawaii and had also taken some personal time, but now he was obviously back.

"Hello, Kit, Cornelia." Greg's smile encompassed them both, but his blue eyes focused on Cornelia and remained there.

"We missed you," Kit said. "How'd you do in Hawaii?"

"Not bad. Came in sixth."

"When did you get back?" Cornelia asked.

"Last night."

Cornelia knew she wasn't in love with Greg, but she had to admit that he always got her blood stirring. It was very flattering to know that he found her attractive and wanted to be with her. At forty-nine, he could have had his pick of younger women, yet he seemed to prefer her company.

"Well, we're glad you're home," Kit said. Her gaze lasered in on Cornelia. "Aren't we, Corny?"

Cornelia could feel herself flushing, and she wanted

to kick Kit. "Yes, we are. And I'm delighted you did so well in the tournament."

"Thank you." Greg looked at the table. "Are you two just starting lunch or just finishing up?"

"Just starting," Kit said before Cornelia could answer. "Would you like to join us?"

Greg looked at Cornelia. "Do you mind?"

"No, no, of course not." But Cornelia did mind. She'd been looking forward to a relaxing meal. Now she'd have to be on her toes, because with Kit there, avidly listening to every word, conversation would be a minefield she'd have to carefully navigate.

Their waiter noticed the addition at the table almost immediately and came over to take Greg's order.

Once he'd left them alone again, Greg turned to Cornelia, "I'm glad I ran into you today, because I have some news. In fact, I planned to call you later."

Cornelia knew Kit would be storing up every morsel of gossip. "Good news, I hope."

Greg shrugged. "It *is* good news, but there's bad news that comes along with it."

"Well, come on. Don't keep us in suspense," Kit said.

Still looking at Cornelia, he said, "I've been offered a terrific job in Hawaii."

Cornelia couldn't hide her surprise. He had taken her completely off guard. "That's wonderful, Greg," she finally managed to say.

"Greg!" Kit said. "But that means you'll be leaving us."

"Yes," he said, finally turning to Kit, "that's the bad news."

Cornelia used the few seconds his attention was directed elsewhere to pull herself together again.

She wasn't sure why Greg's news had affected her so strongly. After all, she had never viewed their relationship as anything but pleasant and temporary. "You've accepted, then."

His eyes met hers again. "I haven't officially, but I plan to. It's just too good an opportunity to pass up." This last was said more softly, almost apologetically.

"I'm glad for you, Greg," she said, meaning it. But she would miss him. Funny that she hadn't realized how much she had begun to count on him as a good friend. And, if she were being completely honest with herself, as someone who made her feel important…and almost young again.

They continued to discuss the new job and what it would entail until their food arrived. Once again, they fell silent for a few minutes. But after Fred was gone and they'd begun to eat—Cornelia her chicken salad, Kit her tuna tartare and Greg his ribeye special—Greg said, "You know, I'm still wondering why this opportunity came my way. I asked how they'd decided on me, but I never really got an answer."

"Well," Kit said, "obviously your reputation preceded you." She took a bite of her tuna. "Yum. No one does tuna like Paulo."

"One of the other golfers mentioned that a Seattle company was heavily invested in the resort where I'll be working," Greg said. "Maybe that had a bearing on their decision to offer me the job."

Cornelia put her fork down. "A Seattle company? Which one?"

Greg speared a fry. Smiled at her. "HuntCom."

"HuntCom," Cornelia repeated.

Perhaps her tone sounded odd, because Greg frowned

a little and said, "Yes. You know the company, don't you?"

"Know it?" Kit squealed. "Why, Cornelia's husband was one of the founders of HuntCom."

"Really?" he said. "I had no idea."

"Yes, well," Cornelia said, keeping her tone light even though her insides were churning. "It's old news. *Very* old news."

"But you're still *very* good friends with Harry Hunt," Kit persisted.

Cornelia now wanted to strangle Kit, even though she was sure Kit had no idea how uncomfortable Cornelia felt, because Cornelia had never even hinted at her feelings for Harry. In fact, she'd kept the subject of Harry Hunt out of all her conversations with Kit…and just about everyone else. She'd always been too afraid of giving herself away. "Yes," she admitted, because she really had no choice, "Harry and I are old friends."

"Maybe you could ask him why they picked me," Greg said.

Oh, I'll ask him, all right. And that's not all I'll ask him. "If I ever have the opportunity, I will." She picked up her fork again and took a bite of her chicken. But it no longer tasted good. Cornelia knew, without ever having to hear one word of explanation from Harry, that he had done what he did best. He had gotten rid of the competition.

Cornelia didn't know whether to be flattered or furious.

One thing she *did* know. Harry had never intended for her to find out about his behind-the-scenes machinations.

She almost felt sorry for him.

* * *

When Zach and Georgie got back to the office, Deborah greeted Zach with a slew of phone messages. "You'd better call Jonathan Pierce first," she said. "He didn't sound happy."

"That man is a royal pain."

"Don't I know it! He nearly snapped my head off." Deborah made a face and looked at Georgie. "I don't envy you working with that man."

Zach heaved a sigh. "Okay. I'll call him."

Zach closed his office door before picking up the phone. If Pierce was going to be hard-nosed, he might have to be told some home truths.

"I resent the fact that you're handing me off to some second-rate assistant," Pierce said without preamble.

"Miss Fairchild is not a second-rate assistant. She's a top-notch researcher and specializes in evaluations of possible grant recipients. You couldn't be in better hands."

"I prefer dealing with you."

"I'm overloaded right now, Jonathan. Miss Fairchild is taking over all pending evaluations." Zach kept his voice level, but inside he was seething. Who did Pierce think he was? He wanted something from them, not the other way around. If Zach didn't think Carlyle was such a worthy possible beneficiary, he might just tell Pierce to take a hike.

"I would think you'd make an exception for us." Pierce's voice was steely.

And why is that? "I'd like to, but I can't."

"I see. And that's your final word?"

Zach sighed. What the hell was the man's problem? "Come on, Jonathan, be reasonable. I—"

"Be reasonable! I am being reasonable. You're the one who's blowing me off. Maybe we should just go elsewhere."

Zach almost laughed. Go elsewhere? Did Pierce think that was a threat? There were dozens of possible grant recipients lined up, hoping for a positive response from the foundation. And the foundation could not say yes to all of them. They simply didn't have enough resources. "If that's your decision, we'll certainly understand."

If he'd thought Pierce would back down, he was wrong, for the doctor, still obviously furious, said a curt goodbye and hung up before Zach could reply.

Zach just stared at the phone. Sometimes he couldn't believe the way people acted. He wondered if he should tell Georgie what Pierce had had to say, but he quickly decided against it. There'd be time enough after Pierce made his next move. Frankly, Zach had just about had enough of the arrogant prick. He'd almost be glad if Pierce went elsewhere. Let someone else deal with his grandiose fantasies.

Looking through the rest of his phone messages, he saw that his sister had called. Deciding he could use a dose of her good humor and common sense, he called her next.

"Hey, bro," she said.

"Hey, sis. How's it going with Princess Emma?"

"Oh, we're having a fine time today. As a matter of fact, we're baking peanut-butter cookies."

Zach smiled. "She loves them."

"Don't I know it. She also loves the raw dough. I had a time stopping her from eating it."

"I'm surprised you were successful."

Sabrina laughed. "Me, too. That child of yours personifies the word *stubborn*."

"Tell me about it."

"Why I called is, I wondered if Emma could spend the night. I noticed that her shoes are all getting tight on her, and I thought I'd take her shoe shopping tomorrow."

"You're a saint, you know that?"

"You keep saying that."

"Because it's true."

"I'm not a saint, Zach. I just…I don't know. Every time I look at Emma, I realize how much she's missed. *Is* missing."

"I know."

"I mean, everyone worries about Katie, and of course, they *should*. She's still hurting. But at least she remembers Jenny. But Emma…she was only a year old when Jenny died. Her memories are gone."

"I know," he said again.

"If I can give her any of that, I want to. And Peter agrees with me." Her voice softened. "He loves Emma, too."

Zach was eternally grateful that Sabrina had married such a stellar man in Peter Norlund. Peter, a respected radiologist at New York Presbyterian, was exactly the sort of man Zach would have chosen for his sister. Generous, thoughtful, intelligent and kind—he was everything a husband and father should be.

"Well," Sabrina said, "I know you're busy. I just wanted to make sure it was okay to keep Emma overnight."

Once again, Zach sat looking at the phone after terminating the call. Only this time he felt good. In fact, he felt so good he decided everything else on his work agenda could wait. He would surprise Katie and go home earlier than expected. Maybe they'd get in several games of chess.

But first he'd give Georgie a heads-up, just in case Jonathan Pierce called back.

Georgie looked up from her computer when Zach knocked on the doorframe. Zach quickly gave her a rundown on Pierce's phone call. "I just wanted you to be prepared in case he calls back. I'm going to tell Deborah to route him through to you, because I'm leaving for the day."

Her eyes flicked to the clock on the wall for a second. Zach knew she was remembering that he'd told Katie he'd be home by six. It was only four o'clock.

"Okay," she said. Then she smiled. "And don't worry. I can handle him."

Zach smiled back. "There was never any doubt in my mind."

In fact, Zach thought as he rode the elevator down to the lobby level, from what he'd seen of Georgie, she could handle anything.

Probably including him.

Chapter Six

Zach hadn't been gone from the office ten minutes when Deborah buzzed Georgie to say Jonathan Pierce was on the line. "And he's not happy," she warned.

Georgie grimaced. He'd be even less happy after they talked.

She pressed a button. "Georgie Fairchild."

"There's been some mistake, Miss Fairchild," he ground out. "I asked to speak with Zach."

"I'm sorry, Dr. Pierce. He's gone for the day." She waited a heartbeat before adding, "May I help you?"

"Do I have a choice?"

"Look, I get it that you're not happy I'm now in charge of the Carlyle Children's Cancer Center application. You made that very clear earlier today, but—"

"Not happy? I consider it absolutely outrageous that I've been foisted off on some *underling*."

If his voice got any frostier, it would rival the

temperature of the Arctic. She decided not to make a point of the fact he'd interrupted her or that he was beyond rude. Keeping her own voice pleasant, she said, "Despite your reservations, I believe we can work together. Unless, of course, you've decided to withdraw your grant application?"

A long moment pregnant with tension passed before he spoke again. "How long are we supposed to wait before you make a final decision?" he said stiffly.

Georgie stifled the impulse to smile. She knew he wouldn't be able to see a smile, but perhaps he would sense it. "I expect to have my recommendation ready by the end of the week."

"I see."

She knew he wouldn't complain because he had probably thought she'd take much longer than that. "In fact," she added, "I've finished going over all the paperwork given to us so far. Now all that's left is last quarter's financial report, which Ms. Love has promised will be in my hands no later than Wednesday."

"You'll call me immediately upon making your decision."

Now Georgie did smile. "Absolutely. You'll be the first to know."

Pierce said a terse goodbye without thanking her. But Georgie hadn't expected thanks. It was enough that he had been made to realize that he wasn't calling the shots.

She was, whether he liked it or not.

It normally gave Georgie no pleasure to brandish her power over applicants, but in the case of Jonathan Pierce, that rule didn't hold true. It gave her a great deal of pleasure to knock that supercilious man down a peg or two. If he hadn't been such a pain in the butt, she would have told him that unless the cancer center's last quarterly financial report showed some discrepancy, their application was all but approved now. That she was making him wait (and sweat a bit, she hoped) was exactly what he deserved for his immature behavior.

She wished Zach were still here, so she could tell him about the conversation. Instead, she sent him an email saying she'd like to meet with him in the morning. She added the teaser, *to tell you about my conversation with Jonathan Pierce*. She smiled, thinking how much Zach would enjoy hearing about the exchange.

Less than thirty minutes later, her email program alerted her to new mail from Zachary Prince.

If you don't have plans for the evening, he wrote, *maybe you'd like to come for dinner. Fanny made stuffed pork chops. We can talk about Pierce then*.

Georgie was so surprised, she had to read the message twice to make sure she hadn't made it up. She immediately wrote back. *I don't have any plans. What time shall I come?*

A minute later he answered, saying, *Great. Let's say six-thirty. See you then*.

Georgie didn't know what had prompted the invitation, but she'd have been lying if she said she wasn't looking forward to the evening. Now that she had changed her opinion of Zach, she could actually admit she enjoyed his company. And, if she was being completely honest (oh, Joanna would laugh at her!), she did enjoy looking at him.

"Well, you look awfully pleased with yourself," Deborah said from the open doorway.

Georgie jumped.

Deborah laughed. "Sorry. Didn't mean to startle you. So what did the great man say?"

For a moment, Georgie thought Deborah was referring to Zach, and she couldn't think what to answer. But then she realized Deborah meant Jonathan Pierce when she'd said "great man." "He tried to intimidate me by saying he didn't want to work with me...*again*. I guess he thought if he said it enough times—especially with Zach not there to protect me—I'd cower or something."

Deborah grinned. "I've only known you a few days, and I already know you're not the sort of person to cower...for anyone." She shook her head. "Wonder how men like Jonathan Pierce get to be that way? Think they have domineering fathers? Who maybe treated their mothers like serfs? Or maybe treated *them* like serfs?"

Georgie shrugged. "Beats me. I'm no psychologist."

"Well, I'm glad you showed the good doc he can't push you around, with or without Zach." Deborah glanced at her watch. "It's almost quitting time." Looking up, she smiled. "Hey, if you don't have plans for the evening, want to come and have dinner with me and my son? Jack's in Cleveland on business, and it's just me and Kevin tonight. Nothing fancy, though. We're having spaghetti and meatballs."

"Oh, thanks, Deborah, I would've loved to, but I *do* have plans. In fact, I'm going over to Zach's for dinner. He just now invited me. I guess he's anxious for a play-by-play of my phone conversation with the great Dr. Pierce."

"Oh, that'll be fun. You'll get to meet his kids."

Had Deborah given her an odd look? "I've already met Katie. We stopped by the apartment on the way back from our meeting at Carlyle so Zach could pick up some files he'd forgotten."

"How is she? Is she feeling better?"

"She told Zach she was." Yes, that was definitely an odd look. Speculative. Or was she being paranoid again?

Deborah sighed. "I feel so bad for those kids. Katie especially. She's taken the death of her mother really hard. When Jenny died, the other two were really too young to be affected. Well, Jeremy probably remembers her a little—he was three when Jenny first got sick and four when she died. But Emma was just a baby."

"It's sad they lost their mother so young."

"It's heartbreaking, actually." She turned as if to leave, then said, "It's been really tough on Zach."

"I can imagine," Georgie said. "Raising three young children on his own. That's a lot of responsibility. Plus... losing his wife. She must have been very young."

"She'd just turned thirty-four."

Thirty-four. Georgie swallowed, imagining only having four more years to live.

"It was awful," Deborah continued. "Such a sad time for everyone. Jenny's mother was devastated. Jenny's father had died a few years earlier, and Jenny was an only child. Zach has done a wonderful job on his own, though. I really admire him. He's got his priorities straight. Unlike a lot of men, he always puts his kids first."

Had Deborah added that last bit for Georgie's benefit? Oh, surely not. Georgie was imagining things.

"I admire that, too," she said. Georgie couldn't help but think of her uncle Harry, who hadn't put his kids first and had paid dearly for that neglect. But at least he'd wised up eventually and made things right with his sons.

"I do hope Zach will meet someone one of these days, though," Deborah said thoughtfully. "He's far too young to be alone. Besides, those children really need a mother."

Those children really need a mother.

The words seemed to echo in the room after Deborah left.

As Georgie cleaned up her desk and got ready to leave herself, she kept thinking about them.

Those children really need a mother.

Georgie knew, if she had any sense at all, she'd steer a wide path around Zach. He was far too attractive, and the more she learned about him, the more she liked him. *I shouldn't be going to his apartment for dinner. I should have said no.*

Yet, what was the harm? It wasn't a date or anything close. It was just dinner, and his kids would be there.

True, but just yesterday, she'd decided she was going to keep her distance from him. Of course, yesterday she'd thought he was married, and today she knew he wasn't.

Did that make any difference, though? He might not be married, but as Deborah had pointed out, he had three young children who needed a mother—the kind of life that was eons removed from Georgie's.

And if Georgie had learned anything in her thirty years, she'd learned that it was dangerous to play with fire. And her undeniable attraction to Zach was definitely fire. *Plus, aside from all else, he's your boss.* She grimaced, imagining what Joanna would say. Georgie had certainly cautioned *her* about getting mixed up with *her* boss.

If I had any brains at all, I'd run for the nearest airport and hightail it on home.

But since she couldn't do that, and since she couldn't call Zach up and say she couldn't make it tonight after all without looking like an idiot, she would make sure that from now on she would stick to her original decision. She would steer a wide path around him. She would be friendly and helpful at the office, and she would firmly stay away from him at all other times.

No matter how much she might be tempted otherwise.

When Cornelia arrived home from the club, she smelled the flowers before she saw them: an enormous bouquet of hyacinths mixed with tiny white roses. She didn't have to look at the accompanying card to know they'd been sent by Harry.

Darling Cornelia,
I know how much you love hyacinths. Every time you look at them, I hope you'll think of me. All my love, Harry

Yesterday he'd sent her a nosegay of violets, the day before a huge spray of baby orchids, all with approximately the same message. All three selections were out of season and had probably cost the earth. And if she hadn't been dealt a body blow today in the form of Greg's news, courtesy of Harry Hunt, she'd probably be thrilled about the flowers. But she was still reeling a bit by the knowledge that Harry wouldn't think twice about playing dirty, even when it came to her.

And why should he? Ruthless tactics had stood him well in business. Winning was all that counted. Take

what you want by any means, fair or foul. That was
Harry's truth. It was the way he operated. Hadn't he
shown her just how merciless he could be when he'd
threatened to disinherit his sons unless they married
and gave him the grandchildren he coveted? He'd been
deadly serious, too.

She was still thinking about him and trying to decide
how she would deal with what he'd done about Greg
when her cell phone rang. She wasn't even surprised to
see Harry's name on the display.

"Hello, Harry," she said.

"Hello, my dear. How are you this afternoon?"

"Just fine, thank you."

"Did you have a nice lunch with Kit?"

"How did you know I was having lunch with Kit
today?"

"I have my ways."

She heard the smile in his voice, and it hardened her
resolve. "Oh, yes, I know you do." *I know all about you,
Harry. You're not fooling me for a second.* "And yes, it
was a very nice lunch."

"I'm glad. You deserve everything nice. And what
about the flowers? Did they arrive?"

"They did, and they're lovely. Thank you. But you
really shouldn't send flowers every day. It's terribly
wasteful."

"It's not the least bit wasteful. Not when they're for
you. You're very important to me."

"Really," she said.

He laughed. "Oh, Corny, I can see I have a lot of
work to do to get rid of that skepticism I hear in your
voice."

"You must admit, I do have reason to doubt you.
Two blonde reasons, one brunette and one redhead, to

be exact." The redhead had particularly upset Cornelia, maybe because by that time she was thoroughly disgusted with Harry's choices. *And hurt. Don't forget hurt.*

"Touché. But it's time for you to forget about the follies of my youth. I'm a grownup now, and I finally know what I want." His voice lowered. "And what I want is you."

A frisson of pleasure rippled through her, even as she reminded herself that Harry had more to answer for than the follies of his youth and that she shouldn't forget it.

"I have a great idea," he said.

"Oh?"

"How would you like to go away for the weekend?"

"Go away?"

"Yes, you know…the two of us…somewhere romantic. Doesn't that sound good?"

"Well," she hedged.

"We could go to Paris…"

Paris. Her favorite city in the entire world. She almost said, *If I do eventually agree to marry you, I'd rather save Paris for our honeymoon.* But something held her back.

"What do you say, Corny? The Eiffel Tower all lit up at night. Montmartre. Maxim's. We could even be naughty and go to the Folies Bergère, if you so desire. And if you don't want to go to Paris, we could go somewhere closer to home. Montreal or Quebec City. What strikes your fancy?"

They all sounded wonderful. But then, when you were as rich as Harry, everything sounded wonderful.

"Let me think about it," she finally said. She refused to allow him to rush her into anything.

"What is there to think about? Which city you prefer? Or whether you're going to go at all?"

"Whether I'm going to go at all."

He sighed heavily, the sound clearly audible over the phone. "All right, Corny. Have it your way. When do you think you might have an answer for me?"

"Why do you need to know? Are you planning to ask someone else if I say no?"

He laughed. "It would serve you right if I did. But no, I've learned my lesson. It's you I want. You and you alone."

She almost said yes right then, but she bit her tongue to keep from saying it. He could just wait a few days. It wasn't as if he had to make plane reservations or anything. Harry's private jet was always ready and available to him, even on an hour's notice. And a few days would give her time to plan just what she was going to say to him about his role in the matter of Greg and his new job.

After telling her he would check in with her the following day, they said goodbye. Cornelia stood there afterward holding the phone and thinking. Was she being silly? Should she just forget all this courtship business and the way he had summarily gotten rid of Greg and tell Harry yes, she'd marry him? Neither she nor Harry were spring chickens. Who knew how many years they had left? Why was she wasting even one minute of them when they could be together?

You love him, faults and all. You know you do.

Yes, she did.

Then there's no reason not to say yes.

But there *was* a reason. Harry had broken her heart once. How could she be sure he wouldn't break it again?

* * *

Now why had he done that? Zach'd had no intention of inviting Georgie to dinner, yet he'd given in to the impulse. And he had to admit that he was looking forward to having her there. Truth was, he liked her. He hadn't thought he was going to, but she'd quickly proven herself to be not only hardworking, with good judgment, but she was smart…and he could relate to her. It also didn't hurt that she was easy on the eyes.

It was kind of a shock that he had noticed. And, if he was being honest, that he'd responded to her. Until now, he'd been attracted to women who were more like Jenny: small, dark, girl-next-door types. No doubt about it. Georgie Fairchild was at the opposite end of the spectrum: tall, blonde and…sexy. Very sexy, because the sexiness wasn't flagrant. But it was there. It certainly was there.

Still thinking about her, he walked into the kitchen to tell Fanny he was having a guest for dinner. He wondered what Fanny thought. She didn't reveal anything of her inner thoughts when he told her, simply smiled and said, "I'll use the good china, then." After a moment, she added, "Will you still be joining the children for their dinner?"

"Until Miss Fairchild arrives." Zach usually ate his dinner early, with the children, but tonight they would be fed first so he could enjoy a more relaxed evening with Georgie.

After he'd freshened up with a shower and changed into jeans, well-worn loafers and his favorite blue sweater—a shade Jenny had always teased him about, saying it matched his eyes—he went back to the family room to check on Katie and Jeremy. He found Katie there alone.

"Where's your brother?" he asked, looking around.

She shrugged. "He got bored. I think he's in his room."

"What're you doing, honey?" The television was dark, and Katie just seemed to be sitting there.

She shrugged again. "Nothing."

He gave her a quizzical smile. "Nothing? Is something wrong?"

"I don't know."

"What do you mean, you don't know? Is your throat hurting again?"

She shook her head. "No. It doesn't hurt."

"Well, then…"

For a long moment, Katie stared down at her hands, which were folded in her lap. When she looked up, her eyes met his almost defiantly. "Fanny said that woman is coming for dinner."

"By 'that woman,' do you mean Miss Fairchild?"

"Yes. Her."

Zach suppressed a sigh. Before Jenny died, he could count on one hand the number of times he'd sighed. Now that's all he seemed to do.

"I don't like her."

"Katie, you don't even know Miss Fairchild. How can you not like her?"

"I don't know," she mumbled. "I just don't."

"But why not, honey? You must have a reason."

Katie didn't answer, just kept looking down and avoiding his eyes.

"Katie?"

Finally she looked up. Zach was alarmed to see tears. "Katie," he said gently. "What's wrong, honey?"

"Are you gonna *marry* her?"

Zach's mouth dropped open. "Marry who? Miss *Fairchild?*"

She nodded miserably.

"Of course I'm not going to marry her. She's just a friend. Someone who is working for me." And yet, even as he said this, he knew it wasn't the whole truth. He and Georgie weren't really friends. They hadn't known each other long enough to be friends. And he *was* attracted to her. Too much so, in fact. Maybe Katie had sensed that.

"I don't want you to marry somebody else." Now the tears had spilled down her face. "I want Mommy."

"Oh, sweetheart …" Zach knelt by the bed. He felt like crying himself. "I know you do. I—I do, too."

"Why'd she have to die?" Katie sobbed.

At times like this, Zach felt so helpless. He knew the pat answers to these questions, but he also knew how unsatisfying they were. "I don't know, sweetheart," he said honestly, putting his arms around her. "Sometimes things happen that have no explanation."

"It's not fair."

"I know it's not fair."

"I miss her."

"Me, too," he whispered.

After a few minutes, Katie seemed to gather herself together, and her tears stopped. "You know, honey," he said, reaching for a tissue so she could wipe her eyes, "Mommy's always with us. I know you can't see her, but she's here. She's probably watching us right now, and maybe, if you close your eyes, you can feel her giving you a hug."

Katie's eyes met his, and he could see she wasn't buying it. She didn't want her mother's spirit. She wanted a real, live mother. And not just any mother. *Her* mother.

Zach sighed again. What could he say to his sweet child to make her feel better? That he would never marry anyone else? Never bring another woman into their lives? How could he promise that? He was only thirty-seven years old. He didn't want to spend the rest of his life as a widower. And he knew Jenny wouldn't have wanted him to, either. In fact, one of the last things she'd said to him before she died was that she hoped he'd meet someone someday.

Finally, not knowing what else to say to his daughter, he whispered, "I love you, Katie. That will never change. You know that, don't you?"

She nodded.

Zach hugged her again, then in a brighter voice said, "Fanny's got macaroni and cheese and tomato soup for you and Jeremy. Do you feel like eating tonight?"

"Uh huh."

"Okay, let's go then. I'll sit with you until Miss Fairchild gets here, okay?"

"Okay."

It hurt Zach to hear the resignation in her voice. Poor kid. She'd barely had time to be a kid before Jenny got sick. Then there'd been the year of treatment, the chemo, the hair loss, the weight loss—all taking place in front of Katie's eyes. She'd had to grow up too soon, experience things no kid should have to experience.

In that moment, Zach knew he could not add to the burden Katie carried. No, he couldn't promise his daughter he'd never marry again, because he hoped someday he would. But he could promise himself that he would never do anything to make Katie feel she came second in his life. And if that meant he would have to be alone for longer than he'd like to be, well, that was the way it was. Unless and until he met a woman his children could wholeheartedly love and accept, he'd just have to accept his own burden of loneliness.

Because his kids came first.

And always would.

Chapter Seven

Georgie had just finished getting ready—she'd changed into her favorite pair of black jeans, a red sweater, knee-high black boots with four-inch heels (she'd take a cab to Zach's, no walking in *these* boots)—and was ready to go out the door when her cell rang. Stopping, she dug the phone out of her bag and saw that it was her mother calling.

"Hey, Mom, I'm just on my way out the door."

"Hi, honey. I was thinking about you and thought I'd check in. See how you're doing."

"Great. I'm doing great. Listen, can you hold on a minute?" Georgie juggled the phone and her bag while letting herself out of the apartment. Once the door was securely closed and locked, she headed for the elevator and resumed her conversation.

"So where are you going?" her mother asked.

"My boss invited me to have dinner at his place. Right now I'm waiting on the elevator."

"Are he and his wife having a dinner party or something?"

"No, it's just me, and there's no wife. But don't worry, it's all on the up and up. He's a widower with three young children. Plus a housekeeper." Georgie wasn't sure if Fanny lived in, but she probably did.

"Oh, really? A widower? What's he like?"

"He's very nice. I wasn't sure I was going to like him, but I do."

"Well, that's good. How old are his children?"

"He's got two daughters, ten and three, and a son. I'm not sure how old the boy is, but I think he's the middle child."

"Oh, that's sad, they're so young. How did his wife die?"

"Honestly, Mom, I don't know. I just know she did."

"What's his name? Is he attractive?"

Georgie rolled her eyes. "His name is Zachary Prince. And yes, he's attractive. But I'm not interested in him as anything other than an employer and a possible friend. So don't get any ideas."

"I just asked a simple question, Georgie."

"Yeah, right. I know you. That was more than a simple question."

Her mother laughed. "No sense arguing with you. I never win. You'll think what you want to think, anyway."

By now Georgie was outside and had bravely stepped off the curb to try to get a cab. Unfortunately, at this time of night, every single cab seemed to be occupied.

Shoot. She should have allowed for that contingency and left earlier.

"Well, honey, have a good time. Call me tomorrow and tell me all about it."

"Okay," Georgie said. "I will. So what's up with you? Anything new?" Deciding to put her mother on the spot for a change, she added, "Seen Uncle Harry lately?"

"Actually, I just talked to him. In fact, I—" She broke off. "Oh, darn, someone's at the door. I'd better go. We'll talk tomorrow."

It wasn't until Georgie had finally hailed a cab and was on her way to Zach's apartment that she thought about her mother's call again. Had her mother wanted something other than to find out how Georgie was doing? For some reason, Georgie had gotten the impression something was on her mother's mind. Well, if there had been, Cornelia would call her again. Because if there was one thing Georgie knew for sure about her mother, it was this: when Cornelia Fairchild wanted something, she doggedly pursued her goal.

As evidenced by the way she is still trying to find a man for me.

Georgie grimaced. Good thing her mother had no clue that Georgie was attracted to Zach, because if she did…she'd never give up. For the first time since arriving in New York, Georgie was extremely glad there were thousands of miles between her and her family.

This way, if Georgie forgot everything she'd decided about steering clear of Zach after tonight and ended up making a fool of herself, at least no one else would ever know.

"And this," Zach said, "is Jeremy."

Georgie smiled at the dark-haired youngster standing

before her. Bright blue eyes the exact shade of his father's stared back at her. In fact, Jeremy Prince was a miniature Zach. He would be a heartbreaker when he grew up. "Hi, Jeremy."

"Hi."

"Your dad tells me you're quite a hockey player."

Jeremy grinned, showing a missing tooth. "I scored two goals in my last game."

"That's great." Georgie smiled ruefully. "I don't even know how to skate."

"You don't?"

Georgie shook her head. "Nope. Where I live, we don't get snow and ice very often."

"You *don't?*" Now he seemed aghast. "Why not?"

"It's not cold enough. Instead we get a lot of rain in the winter."

"I don't like rain."

Georgie laughed. "As a kid, I didn't, either."

"You should come skating with us sometime," Jeremy said. "We go 'most every Sunday, don't we, Dad?"

Throughout this exchange Katie hadn't said a word.

Zach turned to his daughter. "What do you think, Katie? Think we could teach Miss Fairchild how to skate?"

Katie shrugged. "I don't know."

Georgie noticed that she didn't look at her father.

"I bet I could teach you to skate," Jeremy said proudly. "I'm the best skater in our family."

"I'm just as good as you are," Katie said, glaring at her brother.

"So do you wanna?" Jeremy said to Georgie. He ignored his sister. "It's a lotta fun."

Georgie was trying to think how to answer that

wouldn't embarrass Zach or put him on the spot when he said, "You're welcome to join us anytime, Georgie."

"Thank you. Maybe one of these days I'll take you up on the invitation." But she knew she wouldn't. She could feel the hostility coming off Katie. *She doesn't like me.* The thought made Georgie feel bad. She would have liked to be friends with Katie, because she thought she understood how the child felt. After all, they had something important in common. Georgie had been barely two years older than Katie when she'd lost her father.

"Now that we've settled that," Zach said, "it's time for you two to get ready for bed."

Georgie was impressed that neither Katie nor Jeremy argued or tried to wheedle their father into changing his mind. Instead, with a polite good-night from Katie and a big grin from Jeremy, they gave Zach a kiss and headed for their respective bedrooms.

"They're nice kids," she said to Zach once they were gone.

"They are."

"I'm sorry I didn't get to meet Emma, though."

Later, during dinner, Georgie thought about how different his life was from hers. The strange thing was, though, that she felt more than a twinge of envy. Distracted and more than a little unsettled by this discovery, she had a hard time pretending to have a good time during dinner.

"Is something wrong?" he asked when she picked at her dessert, a really luscious apple tart.

She quickly shook her head. "Oh, no, everything was wonderful. Fanny's a marvelous cook. I'm just too full... and a bit tired."

He smiled. "A new job, a new city, new hours… I'm not surprised."

She nodded. "If you don't mind, I'm going to head on home now. Thank you again for inviting me."

"My pleasure."

Zach walked her out to the foyer, where she retrieved her coat, scarf and gloves from the coat closet. As she buttoned her coat, he said, "You know, I was worried when Alex told me you were coming to work at the office."

"Really?" She wound her scarf around her neck. "Why?"

He shrugged. "Friend of the Hunt family and all that…I didn't know what to expect." He laughed softly, almost in embarrassment. "I wondered if you were coming to spy on me."

"Alex would never do anything like that." And yet hadn't *she* wondered about Alex's motives herself?

"But I've been very pleasantly surprised," Zach said warmly.

Georgie's heart gave an unwelcome lurch as her eyes met his. She couldn't think what to say.

"I think we're going to make a good team."

"I—I do, too."

"And I'm very glad you're here."

Georgie swallowed. There was a look in his eyes she couldn't define. Whatever it was, it was making her heart thud—too fast and too loud. God, he had gorgeous eyes. For a moment, she continued to stand there, feeling like a tongue-tied fool. *I'd better get out of here.* Finally she said, "Thanks again, Zach, for a great evening. Good night."

"'Night, Georgie." He held the door open for her. "Don't forget. Let the doorman call a cab for you."

"I will."

"Don't even think about walking home alone."

"No, I won't."

"See you tomorrow."

More than anything, she wanted to turn around and see if he was watching her as she walked away, but she forced herself to go to the elevator without looking back. Only when the elevator dinged its arrival did she glance over to the entrance to his apartment. Zach stood there in the open doorway, and when their eyes met, he raised his hand in farewell.

She smiled, raised hers in return and entered the elevator.

She felt…she didn't know how she felt. As if she'd run a marathon or something. As if she'd climbed a mountain and had finally reached the top. As if all the oxygen had suddenly been zapped from the air.

She was actually trembling. Geez Louise, what was *wrong* with her? She kept remembering the way Zach had looked at her when he'd said they made a good team, that he was glad she was there. And then, like a bucket of ice water, she remembered the way his daughter had looked at her. Then she remembered Deborah's warning, for that's the way she was beginning to think of what she'd said: *Those children really need a mother.* And finally she remembered Joanna and the reckless way she'd taken up with a man who was completely wrong for her.

Don't be like Joanna. You know Zach isn't for you. No matter how attractive he is, no matter how attracted to him you are, he isn't for you. You need a Mr. Right-Now, someone sexy and attractive to flirt with and possibly have a fling with while you're in New York. Zach is the opposite of that—he's a Mr. Commitment, with three children who need a mother. And even if you were willing to consider being that mother someday—which she wasn't*—his oldest child doesn't like you.*

How could Zach possibly fit into her life? Or her into his? Was she ready to give up her job and move to New York? Ready to stop traveling around the world? Ready to assume responsibility for a ready-made family?

No, she wasn't.

So she needed to put his sexy smile and gorgeous eyes right out of her head, and then she needed to run as far and as fast as her legs would carry her.

Because Zachary Prince might as well be wearing a big red sign saying Danger Ahead.

Cornelia finally made up her mind. And she did it without consulting anyone. She'd thought she might bounce her idea off Georgie, see what her oldest daughter had to say, but Georgie had obviously had other things on her mind when Cornelia called her, so in the end, Cornelia made her own decision. Still, talking to Georgie hadn't been a waste, because the conversation with her oldest daughter had given Cornelia an idea.

Picking up the phone, she called Harry.

"About time," he said. "I was beginning to think you were just going to ignore me, not give me any kind of answer at all."

"Now, Harry, you should know me better than that."

He chuckled. "I do, Corny. I was just trying to get a rise out of you."

She smiled. "I've made a decision."

"I hope it's a favorable one."

"I've decided that yes, I'd love to go away with you this weekend."

"Wonderful. What's it to be? Paris? Montreal?"

"Not exactly. Um, what would you say to New York?"

"New York? But, Corny. It's February."

"It's February in Paris and Montreal, too."

"But what does New York have that Paris doesn't?"

"Georgie," Cornelia said without a moment's hesitation.

"Ah. I see. You're missing your girl."

"Something like that. I just thought…as long as we're going somewhere…I could kill two birds." She didn't dare tell him she wanted to check out this boss of Georgie's, this young widower. Especially since she'd gotten onto Harry's case when *he'd* meddled in her daughters' love lives. Oh, Harry would have a field day if he knew what she was thinking.

"Tell you what. Why not really kill two birds?" he countered. "How about if we go to New York tomorrow, stay over a night or two so you can see Georgie, then on the weekend fly to Paris. We could stay there two or three nights—have a real Valentine's Day weekend, then come back home. That way you can see Georgie *and* Paris."

"You know, if we're going somewhere after New York, I'd rather go somewhere warm," Cornelia said. She was still thinking about that Valentine's Day remark he'd made. "We can save Paris for a possible future trip. How about the Keys? I've never been to Key West."

"You know, Corny, you never cease to surprise me. Key West would be about the last place I'd ever imagine you wanting to go."

"And why do you say that?" Cornelia wasn't sure whether to be flattered or insulted.

"Key West just doesn't seem like your style."

"Well, Harry, for your information, I know how to let my hair down as well as the next person. In fact, I may just surprise you." She actually had more than one surprise for him.

He laughed. "Is that a promise? Or a threat?"

"You figure it out."

But she was laughing, too, when they hung up. She was actually looking forward to this.

Thursday morning at eleven o'clock, Georgie had picked up the phone to call Jonathan Pierce when Deborah buzzed her. "Georgie, you've got some visitors."

"Visitors?" Who in the world would come here to see her? Surely not the great Dr. Pierce.

"I think you should come out and see for yourself," Deborah said.

Frowning, Georgie got up and walked out to the reception area, where she promptly did a double-take. Standing there by Deborah's desk were the last two people on earth she'd ever imagined would be there: Harry Hunt and her mother, Cornelia, both of them looking like the cat that ate the canary's grant application.

"Surprised, darling?" her mother said, walking forward to give her a hug and kiss.

"Stunned," Georgie said. Her mother's cheek was still cold from the freezing weather outside. Georgie's eyes met Harry's dark ones over her mother's shoulder. "What are you two doing here?"

"Just visiting for a couple of days," Harry said. "Then we're off to Key West."

"Key West? Seriously?" Georgie gave her mother a quizzical look. "What's up?"

Cornelia smiled. "Just a little vacation."

"Really?" Georgie was still stunned. Did this mean her mother and Harry were actually dating now?

"I really wanted to take her to Paris," Harry said, "but she said she'd rather go somewhere warm."

"I don't blame her for that," Georgie said, grimacing. "I'd rather be somewhere warm myself." They must be dating. Georgie could hardly wait to tell her sisters. She wondered if they knew about this trip. They must not, otherwise surely one of them would have called her.

"Me, too," Deborah said.

Belatedly, Georgie remembered Deborah's presence. "Deborah," she said, "you know Mr. Hunt, don't you?"

Deborah smiled. "I've had the pleasure."

Harry beamed at her.

"And this is my mother, Cornelia Fairchild."

"I'm so pleased to meet you," Deborah said. The two women shook hands.

Always attractive and well-dressed, today Georgie's mother looked absolutely beautiful. Her face glowed, whether from pleasure or the outside cold, Georgie didn't know, but it really didn't matter. Cornelia wore a raspberry cashmere coat and matching hat, with a creamy wool scarf and black leather gloves. Black leather boots encased her slim legs, and her eyes sparkled.

She looked so happy. Georgie realized it had been a long time since she'd seen her mother look this way. Cornelia was always pleasant and seemed content, but she'd never looked like someone had just given her the moon. Georgie knew that was a fanciful thought, but she couldn't think of any other way to describe her mother's glow. She actually looked lighted from within. This must be Harry's doing. Had things between her mother and Harry progressed more rapidly than Georgie and her sisters knew? Georgie hoped so. Her mother deserved to be happy, and if Harry was the person she wanted, then Georgie wanted him for her.

"Is Zach here?" Harry asked.

"No," Deborah said. "He had an appointment with the accountant. But I expect him back any time."

Harry looked at his watch. "We can wait, don't you think, Cornelia?"

"Certainly. I'll visit with my daughter."

Turning to Deborah, Harry said, "We want to take Zach to lunch with us. And you are welcome, as well."

"Thank you. I'd love to go."

"While we're waiting, I'll make a few phone calls," Harry said.

"You can use the office next to Georgie's," Deborah said.

Once he was settled into the vacant office, Georgie invited her mother into hers and gestured to one of the two extra chairs in the room.

"So you're going to Key West?" she said.

Her mother smiled. "Yes, I'm excited."

"Why Key West?"

Cornelia shrugged. "I don't know. I just think it seems so romantic or something. I've always wanted to go there." She grinned. "Actually, Harry did want to take me to Paris. I think he's disappointed."

"No wonder," Georgie said dryly. It was no contest between the two cities, in Georgie's opinion. Of course, Georgie had never been to Paris, and her mother had. "So why New York first?"

"I wanted to see you."

"Why? I've barely been gone two weeks."

"I know, but I wanted to see where you're living. And—"

"And, what?"

Cornelia hesitated. "And I wanted to meet your boss."

"Mother! I thought we settled this."

"Don't look at me like that, Georgie. It's not what you think."

"How do you know what I'm thinking?"

"Because I know exactly how your mind works."

"Mom, you promised!"

"Georgie, I just want to meet the man. That's all. He sounds…intriguing."

"I cannot believe this. You made Harry bring you to New York just so you could meet Zach because you think he might be a prospect for me."

"That's not true."

"It *is* true, and you know it." Georgie closed her eyes. "I'm so embarrassed, I could die."

"Oh, stop acting like a drama queen," her mother said. "Why should you be embarrassed? I mean, even if I was thinking about your boss as someone you might be interested in, and I'm not admitting a thing, he wouldn't know it. No one would know it. So why be embarrassed?"

Georgie stood up. She felt like throwing something. Why did her family persist in this kind of behavior? Did they *enjoy* making her life more complicated? "I'll tell you one thing, Mother. I'm not going to lunch with you at all, if that's what you're planning. I won't be a party to this."

"Georgie, don't be ridiculous. You'll just call more attention to yourself by refusing to accompany us to lunch than if you simply go. What do you think I'm going to do? Ask your boss embarrassing questions pertaining to you? Surely you know me better than that."

Georgie wanted to scream. Throw something first, and then scream. Or vice versa. Instead, feeling totally impotent, she sat back down and glared at her mother. Bad enough she was secretly attracted to Zach and having a hard time keeping to her resolution to keep as far away from him as possible, but to have her mother scheming and plotting in the opposite direction was too much.

Cornelia sighed. "I promise you," she said quietly, "I will not, by word or deed, do anything to embarrass or upset you."

Only slightly mollified, Georgie reluctantly said, "Okay. But if you do…"

"I won't." Her mother looked around, her gaze settling on the small framed photo of their family—Cornelia surrounded by her four daughters—that Georgie always took with her on her assignments. Here in New York, the photo sat on Georgie's desk. "How do you like your job here so far, Georgie?"

"It's better than I thought it would be."

"Well, that's good. I—"

Hearing the office door open and Deborah greeting him, Georgie interrupted, saying, "We'll talk later, okay? Zach is back." And of course, the moment she realized this, her stupid heart sped up.

A moment later, Zach stopped in the open doorway.

"Hi, Zach. This is my mother, Cornelia Fairchild. Mother, this is Zachary Prince, the director here at the office."

Zach walked in and took Cornelia's hand. "Mrs.

Fairchild. I'm delighted to meet you." His eyes were warmly admiring.

Cornelia smiled. "Thank you. It's a pleasure meeting you, as well."

"What brings you to New York?"

"Didn't Deborah tell you?" Georgie asked. "She came with Harry. Harry Hunt." Why did Zach have to look so handsome today in his dark overcoat and navy pinstripe suit and with those devastating blue eyes? She knew her mother would jump on the fact that Georgie hadn't told her how good-looking he was. She carefully avoided her mother's all-seeing gaze.

"No," Zach said, looking around, " she only said we had visitors."

From next door, Harry's laugh boomed.

"Ah, I hear him," Zach said.

"He decided to make some phone calls while we were waiting for you," Cornelia said.

"They want to take us all to lunch," Georgie said.

"I'd better make a quick phone call myself, then." Zach held up a pink slip.

Once he'd gone across to his own office, Cornelia leaned forward. Softly, so she wouldn't be overheard, she said, "You didn't tell me he was so handsome."

"I didn't think that was important."

Her mother didn't answer, simply smiled. But the smile said it all. And Georgie knew her mother knew she was lying. Because part of what made Zach Zach was how he looked. And the fact that his looks didn't seem important to him.

Ten minutes later, the five of them were seated in the limousine Harry'd hired—which had been illegally parked and waiting for them while he and Cornelia were in the office—and on their way to Joe Allen's, in the theater district. Harry had said it was one of his favorite places to eat, and Zach agreed, saying it was a good choice.

Harry had called ahead, so they had a table waiting for them when they arrived. Georgie liked the look of the restaurant immediately, casual and comfortable. As they took their places, Georgie was glad Deborah was with them, otherwise she might have felt awkward, almost as if she and Zach were a couple, which they absolutely were *not*. As it was, Deborah was seated next to him, and Cornelia was on his other side. Georgie sat between Deborah and Harry.

After they'd ordered—with Harry insisting on a bottle of wine for the table—Harry asked Zach what they were working on.

"Aside from the Carlyle Children's Cancer Center, which is wrapping up," Zach said, "we have two other projects under active consideration. One—a literacy project in Appalachia—was suggested to us by Jennifer Rogers."

"A good woman," Harry said.

"Yes."

"I'm hoping to work on that project before I leave," Georgie interjected.

"And the other is the Fielding Institute," Zach said. "They're at the top of our priority list right now because they've been waiting the longest."

Harry thought for a moment. "They do Alzheimer's research, right?"

"Right."

"What about applications? How are they running?"

Zach sighed. "Ask Georgie. She's got a stack on her desk, and there are more every day. It's impossible to keep up. We could work 'round the clock, and I'll bet we still couldn't stay current. Fact is, the last few years have been hard on everyone, and we can only help so many."

They talked about the foundation for a while longer, then Harry, who was always interested in people, asked Deborah to tell him about herself.

Deborah smiled. "I'm pretty boring."

"Somehow I doubt that," Harry said, giving her the full treatment of his famous smile.

"Trust me, I am. Here's my life in a nutshell. Graduated cum laude from Barnard. Married to an engineer. One son, nine years old."

"That doesn't sound boring at all," Cornelia said. "That sounds like a full and satisfying life." Her eyes met Georgie's across the table.

Unlike mine, Georgie thought. She knew exactly what her mother was thinking.

"And I understand you have three children," Cornelia said, smiling at Zach.

"Yes, and they're a handful."

"How old are they?"

"Katie is ten, Jeremy is seven and Emma is three going on ninety-three."

Cornelia laughed. "I used to say the same thing about Georgie."

"Emma is adorable," Deborah said. "Kevin—that's my son—thinks she's great. He keeps asking me when *we're* going to get a baby sister."

Zach made a face of mock alarm. "I hope not anytime soon. I can't afford to lose you, too. Not even for a few months."

"He's a slave driver," Deborah said to Harry. "Tote that barge. Lift that bale."

They all laughed.

"How is that search for a new assistant coming along?" Harry asked.

Zach was just about to answer when their waiter approached with their food. He waited until they'd been served, then said, "I had a promising call this morning. This guy worked for United Way in D.C., but his wife was offered a terrific opportunity here in Manhattan—something they felt they couldn't turn down—so now he's looking. We had a long talk, and I really liked him. He's coming in to interview tomorrow morning."

Turning to Deborah, he added, "Keep your fingers crossed."

Georgie knew she should be happy. If Zach hired this candidate, that meant she'd be leaving New York in a matter of weeks. *And isn't that what you wanted? To get back to doing what you do best? Free and unencumbered?*

Of course it was. This was exactly what she'd hoped would happen. Exactly what Alex had told her would happen.

Why then did the thought of leaving the New York office suddenly make her feel so empty? And so much like crying?

Chapter Eight

"That was a lovely lunch," Cornelia said. "Probably the best salmon I've ever had outside of Seattle."

"It *was* good," Georgie said. She'd also ordered the salmon.

"I love their food," Deborah said. "Whenever Jack and I have something to celebrate, we invariably come here."

As they all rose to leave, Zach turned to Georgie and said, "Since your mother's in town, Georgie, why don't you take the rest of the day off?"

"Yes, darling, do," Cornelia said.

"But there's so much to do," Georgie said.

"It'll be there tomorrow," Zach said.

Georgie had wanted to talk to Zach about a phone call she'd had that morning, but she guessed it could wait. "Okay. You twisted my arm."

Later, after Harry had dropped Georgie and her

mother at Georgie's apartment and gone on to the office with Zach and Deborah, Cornelia said, "I really like Deborah and Zach, Georgie. They are both very nice people."

"Yes, they are."

"You'll miss them if Zach hires this new man and doesn't need you anymore."

"That's probably true."

Cornelia seemed to consider, then quietly said, "Maybe *you* should think about applying for the job yourself."

Georgie sighed. "Mother, honestly, you couldn't be any more transparent."

"What do you mean?" her mother said innocently.

"You know exactly what I mean. But you might as well put that idea out of your head, because I have no interest in applying for the job. I work in the field. I love working in the field. I have no intention of giving it up."

For a long moment, her mother didn't say anything. When she did, her voice was resigned. "You're so stubborn, Georgie. You'd cut off your nose to spite your face."

Georgie opened her mouth to retort, then decided it was useless. She and her mother were miles apart in their thinking. They would never agree. So why waste her breath?

And yet...there was something about her mother's suggestion that had, just for a brief moment, seemed extremely appealing.

But why would she want to give up her lucrative position as a field agent, with all its challenges and freedom, to be cooped up in a small office in New York?

Especially when she'd already figured out that any kind of relationship with Zach was out of the question.

It might be different if he were free…single and un-encumbered. But he wasn't. So even though it made her feel bad to think about leaving so soon, just as she was beginning to enjoy being here awhile, Georgie knew that the best possible thing that could happen would be for Zach to hire the man he was interviewing in the morning.

Then she could go back to Seattle and forget about New York…and everyone in it.

Friday morning Luke Peterson showed up for his ten o'clock interview fifteen minutes early. Zach liked that. It showed the man was eager. Slim and athletic-looking, Luke was an all-American type with thick, sandy-colored hair and friendly hazel eyes. He had a firm handshake and a nice smile. Zach liked him immediately and knew he would be a good people person—an essential characteristic for a job like this.

Luke had a terrific background. He would be an asset to the office, any office. He was just the kind of candidate Zach had hoped they would get but was afraid they wouldn't. Ten minutes after they began talking, Zach knew he'd found his new assistant. But he went through the process, anyway, because it wouldn't be right not to.

"C'mon, I'll introduce you to the others," Zach said when they'd finished going over the responsibilities of the position. First he took Luke out to formally present him to Deborah, who, after talking to Luke for a while, gave Zach a thumbs-up behind Luke's back.

Zach smiled and then took Luke to Georgie's office. Zach felt a pang at the realization that finding Luke meant losing Georgie, but if he was being realistic, he knew Georgie—no matter how appealing—could never have been a permanent part of either the New York office or Zach's life. Their worlds were simply too far apart.

"Georgie, I want you to meet Luke Peterson," he said. Georgie got up from her desk and walked around to shake Luke's hand. Zach noted that she looked particularly nice today in a black pencil slim skirt and white silk blouse.

"What do you think of New York so far?" she asked Luke after they'd chatted a minute or two.

He smiled. "I like it. Of course, I've spent quite a bit of time here in the past, so it's not like it's new to me. When I was with United Way, I came to New York often for meetings."

"So this won't be a stretch for you."

"No, not at all."

Georgie's eyes met Zach's, and he could see she approved of Luke. Again, he felt that pang. He would miss her. She hadn't been there long, but already she was an integral part of the place. He would miss her a lot.

Back in his office, he said to Luke, "I'll need to verify your references, but if everything checks out the way I expect it to, the job is yours if you want it."

Luke nodded. "I'm very interested. But I have to be honest with you. I have two other interviews—one this afternoon and one on Monday."

"I see."

"Right now, though, you're at the top of the list."

"I'm glad to hear it. Do you have any more questions?" Zach smiled. "Anything at all I can tell you that might help our case?"

"I'm sure I'll have more questions. Let me think about

everything, read through the literature you've given me and I'll call you."

Zach had no choice but to leave it at that. He thanked Luke for coming in, told him again how much they liked him and how much he'd like to have him on board, then said goodbye.

Afterward he asked both Deborah and Georgie to come into his office. "What did you two think of him?" he asked.

"I liked him," Deborah said. "I think he'd fit in."

"Yes, I liked him, too," Georgie said.

"Are you going to offer him the job?" Deborah asked.

"If his references all check out. However, he's interviewing for a couple of other positions, as well."

Deborah frowned. "Where?"

"I don't know. I didn't feel as if I could ask, and he didn't volunteer the information."

"That's too bad," Deborah said. Her frown deepened. "Just about everyone else pays more than we do."

Georgie cocked her head. "Is that still true? I thought the board was raising administrative salaries."

Zach grimaced. "Unfortunately, it's still true. Although you're right, the board is considering raising salaries to be more competitive. But it's tough. The foundation doesn't have enough funds to do everything we'd like to do as it is, and putting money into administrative costs isn't high on anyone's list." He looked at Deborah. "Sorry, Deb. Nothing personal."

"I know. Jack is constantly telling me I'd make more somewhere else. But I love this place and I believe in what we do. Money isn't everything."

Georgie felt the same way. She, too, could probably

make more money elsewhere, but she loved working for the foundation. She wouldn't give it up for anything.

"Luke did say we were at the top of his list," Zach said.

"That sounds encouraging," Deborah said.

Zach shrugged. "I hope so. Anyway, let's keep our fingers crossed and hope he'll decide in our favor."

As Deborah got up to leave, Georgie said, "Zach, do you have a few minutes? There's something I wanted to run by you."

"Sure."

When Deborah was gone, Georgie said, "I know I'm supposed to be concentrating on the Fielding Institute application since they're top of the list, but I came across something else that really intrigues me."

He raised his eyebrows.

"It's not a formal application," she went on. "It's a letter and some photos sent by a music teacher at one of the public schools here in the city. With the help of an alumnus who plays the violin with the New York Symphony, this teacher—her name is Shawn O'Malley—has begun a special program at her school. She's managed to get some donated violins, and between her and this alumnus, they've been teaching kids to play, with huge success. Apparently, it's made an enormous difference in the kids' attitude toward school *and* in their grades. Unfortunately, though, the program is running out of money, and the O'Malley woman is hoping we might be willing to fund the project."

"We've never done anything quite like that before," Zach said. "As you know, we generally steer the bulk of our funds toward providing food and medical supplies or medical research."

"I know. But I'm really interested in this, and I'd like to look into it further. It seems very worthwhile to me."

He nodded. "Can't hurt anything. Sure. Go ahead." He shuffled some papers on his desk, then his gaze met hers again. "Georgie, if Luke Peterson accepts our offer, I'd still like you to stay on for at least another month, maybe two. Would you mind?"

"No, not at all." Funny how just a week earlier, she would have minded a lot.

"Luke will need to be brought up to speed on the way we do things as well as on the individual applications. I particularly want you to accompany him in the field for at least the first two or three projects. He's got a great background but no field experience."

"Would the Appalachia project fall into that group?"

Zach nodded. "Yes." He fiddled with a paperclip, seemed to be thinking.

He was silent so long, Georgie began to feel uncomfortable.

Finally he said, "I wish Luke's coming didn't mean your leaving."

Georgie swallowed. "I wish that, too," she answered softly. Her heart picked up speed as their eyes locked.

Again, a long moment passed. "We'll miss you," he said.

We'll miss you. Not *I'll* miss you. Georgie nodded and stood. "Thanks. I'll miss you guys, too."

And then she turned and went into her own office, quickly, before her eyes or expression revealed any of her conflicting emotions.

"It looks like I'll be coming back to Seattle soon."

"Really?" Joanna said. "What happened?"

"Zach interviewed a guy today that he really liked, and he plans to offer him the job."

"Well, that should make you happy."

"Yeah. It's what I wanted."

"Then why don't you sound happier?"

"I don't know. I was just kind of getting used to the office. And there are a couple of things I'm working on that I'd like to see finished." She wasn't about to admit how confused she felt. Not even to Joanna.

"Well, I'm sure he'll have to serve out a notice somewhere. That should give you some time to wrap things up."

"No. No notice. He and his wife have moved to New York from D.C. and he's currently jobless."

"Still…he'll need someone to train him, won't he?"

"Yeah." Georgie knew she should be happy about Luke. But dammit, she wasn't.

"Something's wrong, girlfriend. I can hear it in your voice."

"No, nothing's wrong."

"C'mon, I know you better than that. Tell me. I tell *you* everything."

Georgie sighed. Should she? If she gave voice to what she was feeling, wouldn't it make it all the more real? And what was the point, really? Nothing was going to change, was it? Zach would always be a Mr. Fixed-in-Place-Family-Man. Forcing herself to sound upbeat, she said, "No, seriously, nothing's wrong. This is a good thing. I *will* have to train him—you're right about that— in fact, Zach's already asked me to. It's all going to work out perfectly."

"You're sure you're telling me the truth?"

"Yes, I'm sure. But I do have some other news." And

she proceeded to fill Joanna in on her mother's visit to New York.

"Will wonders never cease?" Joanna said. "And you say they've gone on to Key West?"

"Yes."

"Sounds great, doesn't it? I could do with some margaritas, sunshine and warm weather myself."

"But you have wonderful Chick to keep you warm," Georgie said dryly.

Joanna gave a throaty chuckle. "Yes, there's that."

"Sounds like everything is going well." Maybe Georgie was wrong about Chick. Maybe he really did love Joanna.

"Oh, Georgie, he's just perfect," Joanna said. "I know you had your reservations about him, but I'm so happy."

"I'm glad for you, then," Georgie said. "I hope it all works out the way you want it to. Listen, I'd better let you go. And hey, when you see Bobbie again, tell her to call me once in a while." Joanna was always running into Bobbie at the coffee shop they both patronized. "I mean, surely she can tear herself away from her husband long enough to say hello to her sister."

"I don't know. She's head over heels."

"That's the pot calling the kettle black."

"You're just jealous."

Yes, she hated to admit it, but she was. After they'd hung up, Georgie thought how much she'd like to be "head over heels." She might not want to be married— or even tied down for any length of time—but she sure could use some T.L.C.

And some sex.

Even the thought of sex made her shiver.

Although she knew this was not a place she should

go, even in her mind, she couldn't help wondering what kind of lover Zach would be. *Well, you can wonder all you want, but you're not going to find out. Mr. Out-of-Bounds, remember?*

Later, in bed, lying in a pool of moonlight and listening to the sounds of traffic below, she reminded herself that the faster Zach got a yes from Luke Peterson, the better off she'd be.

Cornelia loved Key West. The city was exactly the way she'd imagined it would be. Harry had booked them into a two-bedroom ocean-front cottage at the Sunset Key Resort located on a private island only a ten-minute boat ride from downtown Key West. It was absolutely gorgeous, but then, she hadn't expected anything less. Nothing but the best for Harrison Hunt.

She'd been afraid that staying in the cottage might be awkward, but Harry made it easy for her, saying she could choose which bedroom she wanted. She decided to let him have the master with the king-size bed. After all, Harry was six feet, four inches tall. He needed leg room. Besides, the second bedroom had a queen, which was more to her liking, anyway. She was grateful that Harry didn't seem to expect her to share his bed, because she wasn't ready.

Cornelia wasn't a prude. Not at all. But she'd been a virgin when she married George, and there hadn't been anyone else since. Maybe hers was an old-fashioned sentiment, but she wanted to do things in the proper order. First a wedding ring, then sex. Her daughters saw things differently, and that was fine. She wasn't judging them. They had their ideas; she had hers. And thank goodness, Harry seemed to respect that. His attitude was definitely a point in his favor.

She still hadn't said anything to him about Greg and his new job. But she would. She was just biding her time, waiting for the right moment. She was no longer upset with Harry. In fact, now she was amused. He must really have been worried or he wouldn't have gone to so much trouble to get rid of Greg. She smiled. Good. She was glad he'd been worried. It was about time he worried about losing her. After all, it was his own fault she hadn't been his long ago.

That night, after a lovely dinner in the resort dining room, and an even lovelier shared bottle of champagne on the screened veranda of their cottage, where they listened to the sound of the waves, Cornelia slept better than she'd slept in years.

The next day proved to be one of the best Cornelia had ever had. They began early, with a wonderful breakfast served to them on the verandah. They drank orange juice and ate strawberries and papaya and scrambled eggs and muffins to the accompaniment of ocean breezes and sparkling water. Afterward, they took the shuttle boat into the city and toured the Little White House—Harry Truman's home—in the morning, had a fabulous lunch at the Pier House Restaurant (the conch fritters were to die for!), then visited the Ernest Hemingway Museum in the afternoon.

Cornelia was enchanted by all the cats at the Hemingway Museum. They were everywhere! Behind trees, under bushes, lying in the grass—just everywhere. Cornelia counted over twenty that she saw personally, and she knew there were many more.

"I think I'll get a cat or two when I get back home," she told Harry after encountering a particularly beautiful calico, who was sleeping under a stone bench.

Harry gave her a funny look. "A cat…or *two?*"

It was only then that Cornelia remembered Harry didn't like cats. He was more a dog person. She smiled inwardly. This would be a true test of his devotion. "Yes. I've always loved cats, but for some reason, I just haven't thought about getting one of my own." She gave him an arch look. "Is that a problem for you?"

"Ah, no, of course not. Whatever you want, my dear, is what I want."

She gave him a beatific smile. "Thank you, Harry. That means a lot to me."

That night they dined at a small French restaurant owned by someone Harry knew, and they were treated like royalty. Afterward, Harry took her to a club where they listened to music until after midnight. Finally, when Cornelia could not stop herself from yawning, Harry suggested they go back to their cottage and get a good night's sleep.

"After all," he said, "we're not as young as we used to be."

"Speak for yourself," she said tartly.

Cornelia sat in the curve of his arm on the boat ride back. "It was a wonderful day. Thank you."

Harry's arm tightened around her. "Every day from now on can be just as wonderful, Corny, if you say yes."

Cornelia smiled. "I know." But she still wasn't ready.

"But I can wait," Harry said. "I can wait for as long as it takes."

When they got back to their cottage, Harry drew her into his arms and kissed her. Cornelia closed her eyes and kissed him back. It felt so good to be held close like this, to be kissed like this. She had almost forgotten how good a kiss like this could be.

That night, as she lay in her solitary bed, Cornelia wondered again if she were being foolish. Was it really wise to make Harry wait like this? He'd said it himself. They weren't as young as they used to be.

But the next morning, she was once again sure of her path. She had also decided it was time to talk about Greg. So, after breakfast and over their second cup of coffee, she said, "Harry, there's something I've been meaning to ask you."

"Before you do, I have something for you." He reached behind him, where a long, flat gray suede jeweler's box lay on a small side table. "Open it," he said, handing it to her.

Cornelia stared at him. "Harry..."

"Open it," he said in a softer voice.

Sighing, she opened the lid. "Oh..." Lying there on a creamy silk lining was a delicate bracelet of small, perfectly matched rubies. Nestled inside the bracelet were two ruby teardrop earrings. They were exquisite. Looking up, she saw the tenderest expression on his face.

"Happy Valentine's Day, my darling."

Cornelia couldn't speak. Valentine's Day. She hadn't even realized it. How long had it been since anyone had wished her a Happy Valentine's Day? She knew how long it had been since she'd had a gift like this. Never.

"Do you like them?"

"I love them," she murmured. Then she got up, went around the table, leaned down and put her arms around him.

He looked up. "I love you, Corny."

Instead of replying, she kissed him.

Afterward, they had another cup of coffee, and he

said, "Before that enjoyable interlude, you wanted to ask me something."

"Yes." She guessed she still did, despite the gorgeous jewels now adorning her wrist and ear lobes.

He smiled at her, his dark eyes gleaming. "Well. Ask away."

"On Tuesday when I had lunch with Kit, guess who joined us."

"I have no idea."

"Greg Berger."

"I see."

"Do you?"

Harry frowned. "I'm not sure what you're asking, dear heart."

"Greg mentioned that he'd been offered a fantastic new job."

This time Harry said nothing.

Cornelia almost smiled. She knew Harry would never out and out lie to her, and obviously he felt staying quiet was the smartest thing to do, especially since he wasn't sure what was coming.

"In Hawaii," she added.

"That's nice for him."

"You think?"

"I would imagine anyone would like a job in Hawaii."

"Is that why you suggested him?"

To Harry's credit, he didn't even flinch. Nor did he look away. "You know exactly why I arranged for him to be offered that job."

"For heaven's sake, Harry. Did you really think it was necessary to get him out of the way?"

Reaching across the table, Harry took her hand in his. His thumb rubbed the back, and his dark eyes never left hers. "I told you before, Corny. I love you. I want you to marry me. And I will do anything it takes to show you how much I care about you. Anything."

Cornelia shook her head sadly. "What am I going to do with you, Harry?"

"Quit being so stubborn and say you'll marry me!" Then, laughing, he rose and pulled her to her feet. "C'mon, lazy bones, let's get going. We've got a lot more things to do while we're here, and time's a-wasting."

Cornelia laughed, too.

What else could she do?

Chapter Nine

Every storefront that Georgie passed on her way to work Monday morning displayed some kind of Valentine promotion. Why was it, she wondered, that you couldn't escape the propaganda? But even as she derided all the hearts and flowers and lacy cards, telling herself they were designed to make money for the merchants who sold them, she knew she would like to be the recipient of something on Valentine's Day, even if it was only a single rose showing that someone cared about her.

Sighing, she told herself that she was lucky to be in New York and so far away from all her friends and family. At least here no one expected her to be showered with candy and roses, did they? In Seattle, all her sisters would be wallowing in the attentions of new husbands and fiancés, and they'd be feeling sorry for her.

But no matter how many times she said it, she

couldn't suppress the feeling of loneliness that refused to go away.

And when a huge vase of red roses arrived for Deborah shortly after nine, Georgie admired them the way she knew she was expected to, but as soon as she could, she excused herself, saying she was loaded down with work, went into her office and shut the door.

Today, she didn't even want to see Zach.

Zach made a formal offer to Luke Peterson late Monday afternoon after both Deborah and Georgie had gone home for the day. On Wednesday, Luke called and said he'd accepted another job.

"I'm really sorry, Zach, but the position offered to me by Warfield March was just too good to turn down." He then told Zach exactly what the offer entailed.

Zach sighed. There was no way he could match the Warfield March offer, which was almost twice as much as the foundation could pay. "I'd be lying if I didn't say I was disappointed, but I certainly understand."

"As much as I would have enjoyed working with you, and as much as I admire what the Hunt Foundation is doing, I've got two kids, and Caitlyn will be going to college in only three years. I've got to think about the future."

Once again, Zach realized how fortunate he was that money wasn't an issue for him. As long as they had the grades, his children could have their pick of colleges.

After they hung up, Zach sat in his office awhile before going out to give Deborah the news. Georgie wasn't there; she'd made an appointment with the teacher who'd started the violin program at her school and would be gone for hours.

Thank God for Georgie. Now that she was taking

so much of the workload off his shoulders, he realized anew how valuable she was. And how right Alex had been.

"Oh, no!" Deborah said when he finally told her about Luke. "He seemed so perfect for us."

"Yeah, I know."

"Darn. Well, Georgie's going to be disappointed. I know she's looking forward to getting back to Seattle."

"Did she say that?" Zach frowned. He hadn't been aware that Georgie was anxious to leave. He'd thought she was enjoying the job. She'd seemed really pleased when he'd asked her if she'd stay on to train Luke if he accepted Zach's offer.

Now Deborah seemed uncomfortable. "Look, she wasn't complaining or anything. It's just that we were talking earlier—before you came in this morning, actually—and I said we hoped to hear from Luke today, and she said, yes, she hoped we did, too. And then she kind of smiled and said it would be nice to have an idea about when she could go home."

Zach told himself that of course she'd be looking forward to getting back to her real life. This had always been a temporary gig for her. Her saying it would be nice to know when she could go home didn't mean she didn't like working for him or that she was unhappy here. It just meant she felt unsettled because her job was temporary.

"The thing is, I think she's lonely here," Deborah said. "Think about it. It must be hard. I don't believe she knows anyone in the city other than us. In fact, after we talked this morning, I made a promise to myself that since it looks like she's now going to be here for a while longer, I would start inviting her to do a few things with me. I haven't made any effort in that direction except for once, when I invited her to dinner. In fact, that was the night she had dinner with you. Anyway, now I feel bad. It can't be any fun for her to go to that impersonal apartment every night, and even though she's independent and all, it must get old eating by herself all the time and going places on her own."

Suddenly Zach realized how self-involved he was. Deborah was right. Georgie *must* be lonely. Why hadn't he thought of that before? He was so busy at night and on the weekends with the kids and all his responsibilities that he hadn't once thought about how alone Georgie must feel, away from all her friends and family and everything familiar. This assignment wasn't like a field assignment, where she was part of a team that worked together, was housed together, ate together and spent their evenings together. Here in New York, she was basically on her own. "You're right," he finally said. "I should have realized all this before."

"You know, I just had an idea." Deborah grinned delightedly. "David's coming to town next week. In fact, he's going to be in the city for at least two weeks. I'll bet he and Georgie would hit it off beautifully. I'll have to get them together."

David Goodwin was Deborah's younger brother and a renowned architect. He was also a former college quarterback, friendly, interesting and extremely good-looking.

"What?" Deborah said. "Why are you frowning?"

Zach didn't realize he had been, and he made a real effort to look pleased about Deborah's suggestion. "I wasn't frowning. I was just thinking."

"About what? Don't you think my idea is a good one? David's always halfway bored when he's here because, let's face it, hanging out with me and Jack and Kevin isn't exactly exciting."

"I'm sure he enjoys spending time with you."

"Yeah," Deborah said dryly, "for the first twenty-four hours, maybe. After that, it's got to be pretty dull. I mean, Jack and I are in bed by ten o'clock! We can't even stay awake long enough to watch the news."

Since Zach couldn't think of any reason at all to quash Deborah's plan, he said nothing further.

Deborah, now that she'd disposed of the problem of Georgie's loneliness to her satisfaction, said, "Did Luke say why he was turning us down?"

"He's going to work for Warfield March. As head of the PR department."

Deborah grimaced. "Well, I guess it's back to square one."

Zach nodded, dispirited on several levels, not the least of which was the picture of David Goodwin and Georgie together, a picture he told himself he had no right to get upset over.

Besides, maybe Georgie wouldn't be interested. For all Zach knew, she had a relationship with someone back home. A woman as attractive and desirable as her…she probably did.

If anything, that thought made him feel worse.

Cornelia thought about her promise to Georgie that she would not meddle in her love life. Did making that promise mean she couldn't speak to Alex about Georgie? It probably did. But Georgie's future happiness and fulfillment meant more to Cornelia than some silly old promise given under duress.

So on Thursday after her return from Key West, Cornelia called Alex.

"Cornelia!" Alex exclaimed when he came on the line. "How nice to hear from you."

"That's one of the reasons I like calling you," she said. "You always sound as if you mean it when you say that."

"I do mean it. You're one of my favorite people in the world. So, how are you? Dad tells me the two of you took a few days and went to New York and then on to Key West."

"Yes, we did."

"And?"

"And we had a marvelous time."

"You know the entire Hunt family is virtually holding its breath."

"And why is that?"

"Now don't play coy. We're all hoping that one of these days you'll become more than an honorary Hunt. I know I speak for my brothers when I say that all of us would be thrilled to have you as our stepmother. And, of course, P.J. adores you, as do all the other wives."

"How *is* P.J.?" Alex's wife was one of Cornelia's favorite people.

"Fat and sassy."

Cornelia smiled. P.J. was expecting her and Alex's first child, due the middle of May. It had been a long road for the two of them. Since they were married, almost three years ago now, P.J. had had two failed in vitro fertilization procedures, but finally this pregnancy had taken. Cornelia knew they were both thrilled and looking forward to welcoming their son.

They chatted a few more minutes, with Alex bringing Cornelia up-to-date on everyone.

Then she said, "Alex, as much as I love talking about

my second family, the reason I called is to talk about Georgie."

"I actually spoke with her yesterday," he said. "She told me she enjoyed seeing you and Dad last week."

"Did she? That's funny, because the whole time I was there, she was irritated with me."

"What for?"

"She thinks I meddle in her love life. Or lack thereof," she added dryly.

"Oh, I think Georgie does just fine in that area."

"Do you? Does that mean she actually has a beau?"

Alex chuckled. "Our generation doesn't use that word."

"Oh, I know. But does she?"

"Not at the moment. At least, not that I know of. She was seeing that doctor she met in Somalia, but I don't think that lasted very long. Long-distance romance and all that."

"So she's free."

"Why do I get the feeling you *do* want to meddle in her love life?" Alex said.

"Because I do. Frankly, I think Zachary Prince would be perfect for her. And she for him."

Alex must have been drinking coffee or something, because it sounded to Cornelia as if he'd choked.

"Sorry," she said. "Did I startle you?"

"You could say that," Alex said. He coughed. "Geez, Cornelia. Give a guy some warning, will you? I mean, you hit me with that right out of the blue."

"Is what I said so shocking? Is there something about your New York director that I don't know? He's not a serial killer, is he?"

"Zach Prince is one of the finest men I know. There's not a thing wrong with him."

"Well, then…I liked him tremendously. I can't think when I've met a man that seems so suited to Georgie."

"But what gave you the idea the two of them might even be *interested* in each other? You do know that Zach has three children, don't you?"

"Yes, we talked about his children when we went to lunch with him. And as far as he and Georgie being interested in each other, it's just a feeling I had watching them together. It was obvious he likes Georgie and she likes him. And he *did* invite her to his apartment to have dinner with him."

"Is that so?" Alex said thoughtfully.

"Yes, that's so. Plus, Georgie acted funny when I asked her about Zach."

"Did she? In what way?"

"I can't explain it, Alex. But I'm her mother. I could tell she's interested in him, even if she wasn't willing to admit it."

"Well, even if it's true that they are attracted to one another, what do you expect me to do about it? They're both adults. They hardly need my help—or yours—to develop a relationship."

"You don't have to do much, but you *can* help. Just make sure she stays in New York for a while. Give them a chance, so to speak. That's all I'm asking."

"Actually, she will be staying in New York longer than we thought."

"She will?"

"Yes. Zach called me yesterday. He thought he had an assistant hired, but the candidate decided to accept another job offer."

Cornelia smiled. "It's fate."

Alex laughed. "Cornelia, you're a piece of work. I thought my father was bad, but you're cut from the same cloth, I'm afraid. Just goes to show that the two of *you* belong together."

Now Cornelia laughed. "We'll see."

For the rest of the day, Cornelia smiled every time she thought of her conversation with Alex. Now if fate would continue to do its part, Cornelia would continue to work on hers.

Georgie was cleaning off her desk Friday afternoon when Zach poked his head in the doorway. "Got big plans for the weekend?" he asked.

She shook her head. "Nothing special. I did think I might go to MoMA. I haven't had a chance to see it yet."

He nodded enthusiastically. "You'll love MoMA. I don't know what special exhibits might be there now, but there's always something good."

"I particularly want to see the paintings by Georgia O'Keefe. And I understand they usually have a van Gogh or two, as well as some of the impressionists."

"At one time they had *Starry Night,* but that might have been on loan from somewhere." He looked at her speculatively. "Are you interested in art?"

"I am, especially modern art. The old masters not so much."

"I'm the same way, have been ever since Sabrina began painting…and educating me. 'Course, I don't get to go to certain museums very often anymore. Most of my free time is taken up with the kids and what they like to do."

"As it should be." Georgie admired the fact that he was such a devoted father. If she were ever to have kids—not that she planned to—she would certainly hope their father would be like Zach. She felt it said a lot about his character that his children were so important to him.

"Anything else on your agenda besides the visit to MoMA?" he said.

"I thought I'd check out who's appearing at Carnegie Hall this weekend, too. Maybe go tomorrow night."

"What about Sunday?" Zach said.

"Maybe I'll just be lazy on Sunday."

"My sister's taking Katie to the country this weekend, and I promised Jeremy we'd go skating Sunday afternoon." Zach smiled. "He wants you to come, too."

Georgie knew then that she should have said she had plans for Sunday, too, but she honestly hadn't thought he was going to invite her to do anything. She'd thought he was just being nice. Making sure she had something to do over the weekend, just the way she'd heard him asking Deborah the same sort of thing. "Well, I—"

"You can't say no. Jeremy would be so disappointed." Zach grinned. "He's dying to show off what a good skater he is."

"What time are you planning to go?" she asked, stalling. She could say she wanted to go to church. Or something.

"Whatever time is good for you. We won't stay more than a couple of hours, probably. Emma gets too tired." He made a face. "So do I. Frankly, *she* wears me out. Besides, it's always crowded on Sundays, even at Wollman Rink. Still, it's fun."

"Where's Wollman Rink?"

"In Central Park. It's where I prefer to go, lots more

room to skate, easier with the kids. And if I say you're coming with us, I won't get an argument from Emma about going to Rockefeller Center instead, so see? You'd be doing me a big favor."

Georgie would love to meet the famous Emma. And skating *did* sound like fun. She'd always wanted to try it. "But I don't have skates."

"No problem. You can rent skates at the rink."

Oh, heck. Why *shouldn't* she go? It's not like this would be a date or anything even close. It would be broad daylight, and at least two of his kids would be there. There was no reason to refuse. "Okay, then. I'd love to go. Want to set a time now, or do you want to call me Sunday morning and let me know?"

"Tell you what. I'll grab a cab and we'll stop by for you around noon. I'll call you when we're a block or two away. We'll go and have some lunch first, then we'll skate."

"It's not necessary to pick me up, Zach. I can just meet you at the rink. I'm sure I can find it."

"C'mon, Georgie, don't give me a hard time. The kids love going to lunch, and they'll both be disappointed if you don't come with us. Heck, I will be, too."

When he put it that way, how could she say no?

Later, as Georgie left the office and walked to the apartment she was now beginning to think of as home, she told herself once again that there was absolutely no harm in the coming Sunday excursion, and certainly no danger. In fact, she couldn't imagine why she'd been so sure she could not spend any time outside of office hours with Zach and his kids. Now if she and Zach were going to be *alone,* that would be different. There was absolutely too much awareness between them to spend even one minute alone with him in any environment other than the office. But lunch and skating with him and the kids on a Sunday afternoon didn't fall into that category at all. Sunday would be innocent fun.

Even so, all Friday night, as she had dinner with an old school friend who lived out in one of the suburbs and had gotten in touch earlier in the week, she kept thinking about Sunday. It was hard concentrating on what her friend had to say, because innocent excursion or not, she got butterflies every time she remembered where she'd be Sunday afternoon and who she'd be with.

Saturday wasn't much better. Exasperated with herself—why *did* she keep thinking about Zach?—she cut her afternoon at MoMA short and took a long walk in Central Park instead. It was actually a nice day, cold but sunny, and she felt a lot better after the physical activity.

She even managed to put Sunday and Zach out of her mind for a few hours that evening because she rented a movie she'd been wanting to see and ate takeout Chinese while watching it.

But later on, in bed, thoughts of Zach came rushing back. And that night, she dreamed of him. In the dream, they were in some kind of outdoor pavilion and they were dancing. Georgie didn't even like to dance, but in her dream she was wonderful, good enough to be on one of those dancing reality shows, and Zach was equally good. They were all dressed up—he wore a black tux and she wore a shimmery sequined gown in a shade of green that matched her eyes.

They were slow-dancing, and he was holding her close. Because she was so tall as well as wearing heels, his lips were close to her temple, and she could actually feel his breath. He smelled wonderful, a combination of his woodsy aftershave and sexy male.

When their dance was over, they stayed on the floor and he kissed her—a long, deep kiss that traveled from her lips down through her body to her toes. It stole her breath and melted her bones and made her heart thunder in her chest. She wanted the kiss to go on forever.

She woke up with the feel of his lips still on hers. She was trembling from the force of the desire the dream had wakened.

What was *wrong* with her?

Why did she continue to think about Zach in ways that only made her situation worse? As a potential lover, he was totally off limits. *You know that!* No amount of wishing would make it otherwise.

Georgie was a disciplined woman. When she decided she wanted something, she went after it wholeheartedly, and she usually reached her goal. The same went for getting rid of bad habits. She'd briefly flirted with smoking cigarettes when she was in college, but when she decided she wasn't going to smoke anymore, she quit, cold turkey. And when she decided in her sophomore year of college that she was gaining weight she didn't want, she increased her exercise and decreased her food intake until her weight stabilized where she thought it should be.

So this inability to wipe something—well, *someone*— out of her mind when she told herself she would, was frustrating. And fantasizing about kissing that someone and having sex with that someone, when kissing him and having sex with him was the last thing in the world she'd ever be doing, was just plain ridiculous.

She was reminded of her favorite book in the world, *Pride and Prejudice,* and how Darcy at one point is furious with himself and vows that "he will conquer this."

I, too, will conquer this. Even if it kills me.

And, she thought ruefully, if the unfulfilled, almost painful ache in her body was any indication, it just might.

Chapter Ten

Georgie dressed warmly, putting on a thick pair of tights topped by a below-the-hip cable-knit sweater. Over that she wore a quilted down car coat. The outfit might not be glamorous, but if she fell on her backside, she wanted some protection.

Her phone rang at 11:55 a.m. "We're about a block away," Zach said. "We'll be out front in just a few minutes."

"I'm ready. I'll be waiting at the curb." Butterflies beat soft wings in her stomach.

"Oh, you're a mess, Georgie Fairchild," she muttered as she waited for the elevator. "If you're going to conquer this obsession you seem to have for Zach, you're going to have to do better than this!"

When the elevator arrived, it was empty, and for that she was grateful. She took deep breaths as she rode down to the lobby level, and by the time she walked outside, she felt more in control. The cab bearing Zach, Jeremy and Emma pulled up about five seconds later.

Smiling at her, Zach got out to let her in. He was dressed casually in jeans and a navy pea jacket with a long scarf knotted around his neck. Georgie wanted to stay cool, calm and collected, but the moment she saw him, her heart skidded and she remembered every moment of her dream the night before. Thank goodness he couldn't know what she was thinking.

"Twins," she managed to say breezily, holding up the ends of the long scarf knotted around her neck.

He grinned.

There ought to be a law against looking as good as he did. In the bright winter day, his eyes were as brilliant as blue topaz. More than anything, what Georgie wanted at that moment was to throw her arms around his neck and kiss him. She had to look away so he wouldn't see the hunger in her eyes.

"Hi, Georgie," piped up Jeremy as Georgie entered the cab. "This is Emma."

An angelic-looking toddler with curly hair sat on Jeremy's lap. Emma's huge eyes, just as blue as her dad's and brother's, met hers. "Hi, Georgie," she said in a high, sweet voice.

By now Zach had gone around and gotten in the other side of the cab and heard Emma's greeting. "Emma, her name is Miss Fairchild. You know that. I told you so this morning."

"Jare-mee calls her Georgie," Emma said. Her entire stance seemed to say she dared her father to dispute that.

So she wasn't as angelic as she looked. Georgie had to bite her lip to keep from laughing.

"And Jeremy isn't supposed to," Zach said, giving his son an admonishing look.

"It's okay, Zach, honestly," Georgie said. "I prefer to be called Georgie. Miss Fairchild makes me feel old."

"See, Dad?" Jeremy said.

"See, Dad?" Emma repeated.

Now Georgie did laugh. She couldn't help it. And when her gaze met Zach's, she could see he was laughing, too, although trying not to. "I'm outnumbered," he muttered under his breath.

"I'm afraid you are," Georgie agreed. She realized she probably shouldn't have contradicted him, but it was too late now. She was just glad he wasn't irritated with her. A lot of men might have been, but Zach had already shown her that he didn't feel his manhood was threatened by a woman's disagreeing with him. And he had a sense of humor, thank goodness. Which Georgie was sure he needed—what any parent needed.

Zach gave the cab driver their destination, which Georgie learned was a place called Ellen's Stardust Diner.

"Do you know it?" Zach said, settling back in the seat.

Georgie shook her head. "No."

"You're gonna love it!" Jeremy said. "It's really cool. They have these waiters that sing."

"Really?"

"They're good, too. Aspiring Broadway performers, most of them," Zach said.

"And the food is the *best*," Jeremy said.

"The best!" Emma echoed.

"I like the Love Me Tenders." This from Jeremy.

"What are Love Me Tenders?" Georgie asked.

"It's a fancy name for chicken fingers and fries," Zach said.

"What about you, Emma?" Georgie asked. "What do you like to eat there?"

"Sketti! Or Moss!" Emma said.

"Spaghetti or mozzarella cheese triangles," Zach translated.

"I love spaghetti myself," Georgie said. Grinning, she turned to Zach. "And what about you, Mr. Prince? Do you have a favorite dish?"

"I do. It's called Hot Diggity Dog."

Georgie laughed. "Let me guess. Hot dogs."

"And not just any hot dogs. New York dogs."

"Like the ones sold on the street? With sauerkraut?" Georgie had already had a couple of street dogs, which she found irresistible.

"You got it," Zach said.

So when they arrived at the restaurant, which was just as charming and clever as Georgie had imagined it would be, with its retro 1950s decor and happy ambiance, it didn't take long to pin down their order, since, except for Georgie, everyone else had pretty much decided what they wanted to eat. After a short struggle where she almost picked the healthy choice of something called a Whole Earth Wrap, Georgie gave in to the stronger temptation to indulge in the Hot Diggity Dogs with Zach.

While they waited for their food, they enjoyed the upbeat atmosphere and a performance of "Love Me Tender" by the waiters.

"They're singing about my food!" Jeremy said, making a goofy face.

Not to be outdone, Emma imitated him.

Zach just rolled his eyes, and Georgie laughed. She had to admit the kids were fun.

Later, as they were eating, Georgie tried to think of another time recently when she'd enjoyed herself more, but she couldn't. She was trying to decide which of the two children she liked better, Jeremy or Emma. Jeremy was showing off, a typical seven-year-old enjoying having a fresh audience, especially an appreciative one like Georgie, who found him highly amusing and entertaining. And Emma…well, Emma was a delight. Obviously a little spitfire, she reminded Georgie of herself when she was young. She would be a handful as well as a heartbreaker when she hit her teen years, Georgie was sure, but if anyone could manage her, it would be Zach.

Watching him, Georgie realized anew what a great guy he was, and she was filled with regret that she wasn't cut out to be the kind of woman he needed. The words Deborah had uttered were ever-present in the back of her mind: *His children really need a mother.*

The only sour note during lunch occurred when they had finished their meal and were waiting for the bill. Two young women approached their booth, giggling and jostling each other. The taller one, a blonde wearing too much makeup, said, "Oh, Mr. Dempsey, will you take a picture with us?" Before Zach could even answer, the other one, a curvy little redhead, whipped out her cell phone and proceeded to take a photo of Zach.

"Please put that phone down," Zach said. "I'm not who you think I am."

The girls stared at him. Georgie could tell they didn't believe him. "He's really not," Georgie said.

"Whatever," the blonde said. "C'mon, Heather, let's go."

"Does that kind of thing happen often?" Georgie asked as they exited the restaurant.

"Not as much anymore."

Georgie could see Zach didn't want to discuss the incident, so she said nothing further.

Zach looked around. "Let's walk down to the corner. It'll be easier to get a cab there."

"Yeah!" Jeremy said, already beginning to run ahead.

"Jeremy!" Zach called. "Get back here. And Emma, you hold my hand."

"I wanna hold Georgie's hand," Emma said.

Zach smiled. "Looks like you're a hit."

Emma's mittened hand settled into Georgie's as if it belonged there, and when the toddler looked up at her and said, "I like you. Will you paint my nails when we get home?" Georgie knew one thing for sure: She was no longer in danger of losing her heart to Zach, because his daughter had already stolen it.

After they'd rented skates for Georgie and a locker to hold their belongings, they ventured out onto the ice. Zach had to hold Georgie firmly or she would have fallen, because her legs wouldn't stop wobbling.

It was so beautiful out in the open air, though—cold, yes, but bright and sunny and sparkling. The snow on the ground was still fresh enough to be white and pretty, and all the skaters, many of them in gaily colored coats and hats, gave the rink a festive look.

Georgie loved it.

Or *would* have loved it, if she didn't feel so awkward and certain she was going to topple over at any moment. She would have been happy sitting on the sidelines, just watching, for Zach and his two children were good skaters. Even little Emma was pretty steady on the ice, and Jeremy was a revelation.

"Wow," Georgie said to him as she watched him zip around, "you're great!"

"Told you!" he said.

"Don't be a smart aleck," Zach said. But once again, the twinkle in his eyes betrayed him, and Georgie knew Zach enjoyed Jeremy's impudence and Emma's stubborn streak.

"C'mon," Jeremy said, grabbing Georgie's hand. "It's not hard."

"Hey, wait," Zach said. "Let her get her sea legs."

"We're not in the water, Dad," Jeremy said, rolling his eyes.

"It's just an expression, son." Zach looked at Georgie. "They're so literal."

She tried not to laugh but was only partially successful.

For the next hour, Zach (patiently) and Jeremy (not so patiently) instructed her on the proper way to navigate the ice while keeping her balance. After a while, she felt she was getting the hang of it, but she knew it would take a lot of practice—a *lot!*—if she was ever going to be anywhere near as good as the Prince men.

Still, by the time they'd been on the ice about an hour and a half, she was moving along fairly easily, as long as she didn't attempt turns or anything other than straightforward skating…and as long as Zach was there to help if she got in trouble. By then Jeremy was bored with teaching and he was having fun on his own, although Zach insisted he stay nearby. Emma, on the other hand, stuck to Georgie like glue.

"You're doing really well," Zach said, "but I'll bet you're tired."

Georgie hated to admit it, but she *was* tired. And her legs hurt because she'd used muscles she didn't know she had.

Just as Zach was about to call Jeremy, who was skating a ways ahead of them, but still in sight, Jeremy whipped around and sped back to them. Shouting, "Georgie, Dad! I can skate on one leg! Look!" he zoomed right up to Georgie, spun and lifted one leg and in the process made her lose her balance, and before Zach could prevent it, she fell heavily, twisting her right leg beneath her.

Because Emma was so close, she also lost her balance and fell on top of Georgie.

Georgie knew, even before Zach began to help her up, that she'd injured her right ankle, because it hurt like the devil, and she couldn't put her weight on it.

"I'm sorry, I'm sorry," Jeremy kept saying.

Zach glared at him.

Emma started to cry.

"It wasn't his fault, Zach," Georgie said.

"Yes, it was. He was showing off, and he wasn't careful."

"I'm sorry, Dad." Jeremy looked stricken and on the verge of tears himself.

"Georgie's the one you need to apologize to," Zach said. "She's probably sprained her ankle." He put his arm around her so he could support her weight. "C'mon, let's get you over to that bench and get your skates off. If you really have sprained that ankle, it's going to start swelling, and you don't want your skates on when that happens."

Sure enough, her ankle looked swollen and red when Zach removed her skate.

Emma had stopped crying and climbed up next to Georgie. "Does it hurt?" she said.

Georgie nodded. "But it's not bad." It was, though. It was throbbing and she knew she wasn't going to be able to walk on it.

"You can't walk on that foot," Zach said.

"But I have to get out to the street somehow. And you certainly can't carry me."

"I'm sorry, Georgie," Jeremy said.

"It's okay, honey," she said.

"Okay, here's what we'll do," Zach said. "Let's get your other skate off so I can return them. You and Emma stay here while Jeremy and I go to the lockers and get our stuff. In the meantime, I'll call Les, this fella who drives us sometimes, to get my car out of the garage and come and pick us up."

"But—"

"He can stop off at the apartment first and get the portable wheelchair we used when Jenny was sick. I'll call Fanny and tell her to wheel it downstairs and give it to the doorman. After we take the kids home, we'll get you to a doctor. Make sure it's just a sprain."

Georgie marveled at how quickly and easily Zach had taken charge. Of course, it helped that he had seemingly unlimited resources. Within forty minutes, the driver showed up. The wheelchair made it simple to get her to the car—which was actually a roomy SUV—and before she knew it, they were pulling up in front of Zach's apartment.

"I won't be long," he told her. "Just stay in the car with Les, and I'll be back in a few minutes. C'mon, kids. Let's go."

"I wanna stay with Georgie," Emma said, pouting.

"You can't. But you'll see her again after we get back from the doctor's."

Ten minutes later they were on their way again. Zach had thoughtfully brought back a couple of Advil for her, along with a bottle of water. "Are you doing okay?"

"It's not so bad, really."

"I'm awfully sorry about this, Georgie." His eyes reflected his concern.

"Accidents happen, Zach. Please don't blame Jeremy."

He just shook his head. "He needs a good talking to."

In an attempt to get his mind off Jeremy, she said, "Where are we going to find a doctor on Sunday?"

"No problem."

"Really?"

"I called in a favor."

"Oh."

"A college buddy of mine is an orthopedic surgeon," he explained. "He said he'd meet us at his office."

"When did you talk to *him?*"

"While I was taking the kids up to Fanny."

Georgie couldn't get over the way Zach was able to get things done. Alex was the same way. They weren't in anyone's face about it, but they accomplished wonders. For instance, Georgie couldn't imagine either Zach or Alex being obnoxious about it, but it was obvious they were used to quietly organizing things and giving orders and having them followed. And Georgie had to admit, but it was nice to be taken care in such a thoughtful, efficient way.

Zach's orthopedic surgeon friend didn't seem the least put out by having to come to his office on a Sunday. He greeted Zach like they were best buddies, and he was happy to do him this favor.

A stocky blond with friendly hazel eyes, he shook Georgie's hand, saying, "Hi. Jim Douglas."

"Georgie Fairchild."

"Let's have a look at this ankle." His hands were gentle as he felt the ankle, but Georgie couldn't help grimacing. "I'm pretty sure it's just a sprain, but let's X-ray it, anyway."

Fifteen minutes later, reading the film, he said, "I was right, it's not broken." He then gave her instructions. "I'm going to immobilize the ankle with a splint. That's to protect it while it's healing." Turning to Zach, he said, "She needs to rest it as much as possible in the next few days, and she absolutely can't walk on it, so it's going to be crutches or the wheelchair." He smiled at Georgie. "Your choice. Also for the first few days, you're going to need to ice it three times a day, to keep the swelling down." Turning back to Zach, he said, "I'll give you some printed instructions to take home."

Georgie wondered if he thought she were Zach's girlfriend or something. Maybe he thought she lived with Zach. "I live on my own," she said, "and if I can't walk, it's going to be difficult." She couldn't even imagine how she'd get to and from work.

"Don't worry, Georgie, I'll take care of everything," Zach said.

But Georgie *was* worried. She bit her lip, her mind spinning furiously. Maybe her mother could come for a few days. Oh, why did this have to happen?

After they left the doctor's office and Zach had lifted her back into the car—if she hadn't been so upset over the ankle, she would have enjoyed being held in his arms—he said, "We'll get you some crutches on the way home."

He had Les drop him at a pharmacy, and while he went in to get the crutches and the other supplies she'd need, Les circled the block until Zach was again outside.

"Thank you for doing all this," she said once he was back in the car.

"It's the least I could do, since your situation is Jeremy's fault."

"Well, I appreciate it."

Georgie had settled down. She still wasn't sure how she was going to manage on her own, but after some of the things she'd suffered in the past year or two (poison ivy, an infected mosquito bite, an encounter with a snake) during her travels afield, she'd become pretty resilient. She guessed she would figure this problem out, too.

They'd only driven a few blocks when Georgie realized they were going back to Zach's place. "Um, Zach," she said, "I thought Les would drive me home."

"You're not going home."

"Wh-what do you mean?"

"You heard what Jim said. You're not to walk on that foot until it heals."

"But—"

"Look, I've got a huge apartment with an empty guest suite. I've also got Fanny, who can look after you."

Georgie just stared at him. Did he mean what she thought he meant?

"You're going to stay with us until you can function on your own. And I won't take no for an answer."

Chapter Eleven

Cornelia had been looking forward to a quiet Sunday for days. Harry had been keeping her so busy, she'd barely had time to read the daily newspaper, let alone relax with her knitting or keep up with her email correspondence.

Harry.

She smiled now anytime she thought of him. He was trying so hard to please her, to be the man she needed him to be. And knowing Harry, who was nothing if not goal oriented, a man who had never failed at anything he set his sights on, he would remake himself if that's what it took to get her to marry him. Because there was now no doubt in her mind that Harry had finally, *finally,* realized what he should have realized a long time ago: The two of them belonged together. He wasn't just saying it, he wasn't going to change his mind in a month, he really meant it.

He loves me.

Last night, after a lovely dinner and an even lovelier snuggle in front of the warmth of a cozy fire in Cornelia's fireplace, she had almost told him she would marry him. But at the last moment, she had decided to wait one more day. This evening Harry was taking her to hear the Seattle Symphony Orchestra at Benaroya Hall. She would tell him she'd made her decision when he came to pick her up, and then she would wear that magnificent pink diamond ring, which would perfectly match the pale pink crepe dress she planned to wear. She knew he'd been carrying that ring in his pocket, ever since first showing it to her. He was like a Boy Scout, only in his case, he prepared only for success.

She hugged herself, laughing softly. The ring was ostentatious, she knew it, yet she had not been able to put it out of her mind. Why not? she thought now. Just once in her life, why not do something totally out of character and wear that enormous ring proudly?

It was in this joyful, expectant frame of mind that she walked unhurriedly to the house phone when it rang at five o'clock. She was already bathed and dressed for the evening, for Harry was coming at six. Caller ID identified Grayson Hunt, Harry's eldest son, on the other end. Without the slightest premonition of anything being wrong, Cornelia smiled as she answered.

"Gray! How lovely to hear from you. It's been too long. How are Amelia and the children?"

"They're all fine, Cornelia. But I'm afraid I'm calling with bad news."

Cornelia's smile faded, and she went still.

"Dad's had another heart attack. I'm calling from the hospital." Gray's normal take-charge, no-nonsense voice faltered just a bit. "He…he's asking for you. I've sent Walter to come and get you."

Nothing could have alerted Cornelia to the seriousness of what had happened more than that hitch in Grayson's voice. Tears filled her eyes even as she told herself she must remain strong. Tears would not help Harry, and that was all that mattered right now. "Thank you, Gray. Is—is he going to make it?" She could hardly force herself to ask the question.

"I don't know. We're still waiting to talk to Dr. Kedar." Chander Kedar, probably the most renowned heart specialist in the Seattle area, had been Harry's cardiologist ever since his first heart scare three years earlier.

Cornelia's hands were shaking as she said goodbye. She allowed herself only a few moments of terror and regret before mentally shaking herself. She couldn't afford to fall apart. She had to be able to deal with whatever happened. Her behavior was the only thing she had any control over. Blinking back her tears, she reminded herself that Harry's health and their possible future together were in God's hands.

Why did I wait so long to say yes to Harry? Was my stupid pride that important? What was I trying to prove, anyway?

As she walked slowly upstairs to change into something more comfortable and sensible for what might be a long hospital vigil, she prayed that Harry would overcome this the way he'd overcome every other obstacle in his life.

Please God, let him live. If you do, I promise I'll never ask for anything else again.

* * *

Zach called ahead to ask Fanny to make sure the guest suite was ready for Georgie.

"It's always ready, Mr. Prince," Fanny said.

"Is Katie home yet?"

"Not yet, but Mrs. Norlund called about an hour ago to say she'd have her back by six."

Zach looked at his watch. It was just past 5:30 p.m. "If she gets there before we do, ask her to wait, would you? I need to see her." He planned to ask Sabrina to go to Georgie's apartment and gather whatever items his houseguest wanted. He would do it himself, but he figured Georgie wouldn't like him—or any man—going through her personal things.

He looked over at Georgie. She was a trouper. No crying, no hysterics, no whining. He knew that ankle must have hurt like hell. He saw how she winced when Jim had examined her, yet she didn't complain. Now that he thought of it, she didn't complain about much, ever. If she really was lonely here in New York, she sure hadn't let on.

Nor did she complain about any of the people they worked with, even though some of them, like Jonathan Pierce, could be pills. He really liked that about her.

Who are you trying to kid? You like everything about her.

She certainly was easy on the eyes. He wondered if she had any idea how appealing she looked today. Or how she'd made him feel when he had his arms around her while she was trying to get her balance on skates. Or when he'd lifted her into the car.

He wished…

But he broke off the thought. Any kind of personal relationship with Georgie, other than friendship, was out of the question, he'd already decided that. Now, if Katie liked her…

But Katie *didn't* like her.

"We're here, Mr. Prince," Les said, breaking into Zach's thoughts. A few seconds later, the driver pulled up to the curb in front of Zach's building. Walter was on duty today, and he rushed right over to help them when he saw who it was.

Between the two men, they got the wheelchair set up and Georgie into it easily. Zach thanked Les, and with Walter toting the crutches, Zach wheeled Georgie into the building.

Fanny was waiting in the foyer when Zach opened the apartment doors and wheeled Georgie in. She gave Georgie a sympathetic smile. "Sorry about your ankle, Miss Fairchild."

"Thank you, Fanny. And please call me Georgie."

Fanny's eyes met Zach's, and in them he saw not just sympathy but a spark of something else. Something that made him a bit uncomfortable, because he knew she knew exactly what he'd been feeling—*was* feeling about Georgie—maybe from the first moment he'd met her, even if he hadn't been ready to admit it until now.

"Fanny," he said, "I'll let you show Georgie the guest suite while I take care of some things." He'd decided to call Deborah and ask her to go to Georgie's rather than have his sister do it. He figured Georgie at least knew Deborah, which might make it a bit less embarrassing for her. Taking out his cell phone, he was just about to key in Deborah's speed-dial number when the phone in the apartment rang. Since Fanny was busy, he headed for the extension in his office, but then Fanny called out.

"Mr. Price, it's Mrs. Barlowe on the phone."

Zach smiled. He kept in close touch with Toni

Barlowe, Jenny's mother and the only living grand-mother his children had. And he never minded a phone call from her; in fact, he initiated them fairly often him-self. "Hi, Toni," he said.

"Hi, Zach. I meant to call you earlier, but things got a little crazy here and I forgot." Toni managed a senior complex in Fort Meyers, Florida. She'd done so for the past five years, ever since her husband (and the children's grandfather) had died of an unexpected and massive stroke. Poke Barlowe had been almost twenty years older than his wife, who was only in her late fifties now. Jenny had been their only child, and they had doted on her. Now all that love and devotion was concentrated on Zach and his children.

"How are you?" Zach asked. Almost the best thing about Toni, a trait he'd been thankful for since the first time he'd met her, was the fact that he could safely ask her a question like this. She would not keep him on the phone for an hour with whining complaints. Toni was like him; she didn't waste time bemoaning anything. If she had a problem, she dealt with it.

"I'm great, Zach. I called to tell you I unexpectedly got a few days off next week, and I'd love to come and see you guys. Would that be okay with you?"

"Of course it's okay. You know we always love having you." And then, for some reason he couldn't explain, he added, "I'm glad it's not this week, though. I have someone staying in the guest suite."

"That wouldn't have mattered to me. I can sleep on the sofa if I have to."

He knew she wasn't kidding. She'd often told Jenny how she and her three older sisters all shared the same room when they were growing up. "We only had one closet. Imagine that. And one bathroom in the entire house." Then she'd laugh, saying, "But we were happy and we had no idea we were deprived." This last was laced with gentle sarcasm because she constantly marveled at the fact that Zach's apartment contained eight bathrooms and six bedrooms.

They talked for a while more, with her asking about each of the children and ending by saying she'd let him know her flight and arrival time after she made her reservation. After they'd hung up, he wondered what he'd have said if she'd asked about his house guest. Had he wanted her to? Is that why he'd mentioned Georgie to begin with?

What did you think that would accomplish? That she'd give you her blessing if by some miracle you could work things out so that Georgie might someday be a part of your life? Do you need *her blessing?*

Still thinking about the conversation with Toni, he placed his call to Deborah.

"Of course I'll go get Georgie's things, Zach," she said. "No problem. What does she want?"

"I'll take the phone in to her, Deb, and she can tell you. Oh, and take cabs. I'll reimburse you when you get here."

Phone in hand, he walked out of his office just as sounds from the foyer alerted him to the fact Sabrina had brought Katie home.

Katie.

For the first time since he'd told Georgie she was going to be staying with him, he thought about Katie. Filled with foreboding, he walked out to the foyer to greet her.

"Dad!" Katie called when she saw him. Her small face was alight with happiness. "It was so fun! Jinks was so happy to see me!"

Jinks was Sabrina's horse, a beautiful chestnut Arabian gelding, and Katie loved him.

"I got to ride him twice!" Katie beamed. "Aunt Sabrina said I was a natural. Dad, can I get a horse?"

"We'll talk about that, okay?"

"Well, can I at least take riding lessons?"

Zach hadn't seen Katie this excited about anything in a long time. "Let Aunt Sabrina and me talk about that, too, then we'll see."

"But, Dad—"

The temptation to say yes to anything his daughter asked was strong, but Zach resisted doing so impulsively. Once you said yes, you couldn't change your mind. Not easily, anyway. "Katie, I'm not saying yes to anything this important without doing some research first. Okay?"

Katie sighed heavily. "Okay."

Zach's gaze met his sister's.

She smiled. Her dark eyes, inherited from their father, echoed Katie's pleasure in the weekend. "We did have a wonderful weekend," she said. "And Katie *is* a natural."

Katie gave Sabrina a grateful and adoring smile.

"How was your weekend?" Sabrina asked.

"Interesting," he said. He was just trying to figure out how to break the news of the accident and Georgie's presence at the apartment when Jeremy, followed closely by Emma, ran out to the foyer. "Aunt Sabrina! Katie! Wait'll I tell you what happened today." He stopped when he saw the expression on Zach's face.

Zach kept his voice as neutral as he could. Maybe if he didn't make a fuss about the situation, Katie wouldn't, either. "What Jeremy was about to say is, we had an accident while skating today."

Sabrina looked at his two youngest.

"No, not them," Zach said. "Our guest." Out of the corner of his eyes, he saw Katie stiffen, almost as if she knew what was coming.

Then, before Zach could explain any further, the sound of wheels against hardwood flooring made all five of them turn.

When Georgie, holding the phone from Zach's office in her lap, came into sight, she smiled tentatively, looking first at Zach, then toward Sabrina and Katie.

Katie stared at her.

Zach hurriedly said, "Sabrina, this is Georgie Fairchild, my assistant. Georgie sprained her ankle today and she's going to be staying with us while she recuperates."

Katie made a sound that was a cross between "no" and a gasp.

And then, shocking Zach, she fled past Georgie, down the hall and around the corner.

A second later, they heard the door of her bedroom slam shut.

Oh no, Georgie thought. Katie's reaction was even worse than Georgie had imagined it might be. Her eyes met Zach's, and she saw he was stunned. For a few moments, no one said a word, and afterward Georgie thought how that was the first time since she'd met Zach that he'd seemed totally bewildered.

"Oh dear," said Zach's sister. She looked at Zach, too.

He finally moved. "I need to go talk to her. Sabrina, why don't you and Georgie go into the family room and get acquainted?" His attention moved to Jeremy and Emma. "You two go with them, okay?"

Jeremy frowned. "Why's Katie mad?"

"'Cause she wanted to go skating, too," Emma piped up. "Huh, Dad?"

"That's probably why," Zach said.

Georgie of course knew that wasn't the reason Katie had acted the way she had. Georgie had seen the look on Katie's face when she realized Georgie was there and was going to be there for a while. *Oh, God. She hates me.* Georgie wished she could talk to Katie. Wished she could tell her she wasn't a threat. That she didn't have designs on Katie's father. That she wasn't trying to take the place of Katie's mother.

Georgie felt so bad for Katie, because she could imagine how the kid felt. Some of what Georgie was thinking and feeling must have shown in her face, because Sabrina—who had begun shepherding Jeremy and Emma toward the family room—said, "It'll be okay, Georgie. I hope it's okay to call you Georgie?"

"Please do," Georgie said, wheeling herself after them.

"Can we watch TV?" Jeremy asked when the four of them were settled in the pleasant room.

"*May* we watch TV?" Sabrina said. "And yes, I think that would be fine. Unless Fanny has your dinner ready?"

Fanny had walked into the room while Sabrina was talking. She nodded, saying, "Dinner is ready, but it'll stay warm. I didn't know if everyone was going to eat together or if you children are eating first..." Her voice trailed off and she looked to Sabrina.

Sabrina shrugged. "I don't know, either. Um, we have a bit of a crisis. Zach's in Katie's room."

Georgie realized the two women had a shorthand of their own, because Fanny nodded knowingly.

"What's a cry-sis?" Emma asked.

"It's when somebody's crying, dummy," Jeremy said, rolling his eyes. He looked at Georgie to see if she was watching him.

"I'm not a dummy!" Emma said. She punched his arm.

He immediately punched her back, and she started to cry. "You hurt me!"

"Yeah, well, you punched me first!"

Emma kicked him.

He started to kick her back when Sabrina grabbed him and pulled him away from Emma.

"Jeremy. Emma. I want you to stop this right now." She turned to Jeremy. "The word *crisis* does not mean someone is crying. It means there's a problem. And Emma is right. She's not a dummy. I want you to apologize to her for calling her one."

"But Aunt Sabrina, she hit me!"

"What's going on in here?"

The women turned as Zach entered the room. Georgie's heart went out to him. He looked so tired.

"Everything's fine, Zach," Sabrina said. "There's no problem."

Georgie saw the relief on Jeremy's face. Emma, too, quit sniffling and sidled closer to her aunt.

"Is everything okay?" Sabrina asked Zach.

"I hope so," he said. He turned to Fanny. "Is dinner ready?"

"Yes. Is everyone going to eat now?"

Zach looked at Georgie. "Hungry?"

"I'm always hungry," she said in an attempt to lighten the atmosphere.

He smiled gratefully. "What about you, Sabrina? Want to eat with us?"

"Thanks, but Peter and Tommy are waiting for me. We're going to Antonio's tonight, since the cupboard is bare." She looked at her watch. "In fact, I'd better be going."

"Okay," Zach said. "Thanks for everything. We'll talk tomorrow."

Georgie knew Zach's sister was probably dying to know what had transpired with Katie, just as Georgie was, but with Jeremy and Emma there, she wouldn't ask.

"It was a pleasure meeting you, Georgie," Sabrina said. "I hope I'll see you again sometime."

"Thank you. I do, too."

Turning to Zach, she said, "I'll call you tomorrow."

Zach nodded and walked his sister out, but not before saying to Fanny, "It'll just be the four of us at the table, then, Fanny. Katie's stomach is upset and she doesn't want to eat."

"I'll fix her some soup, then, maybe?" Fanny said.

Zach shook his head. "No. She's gone to bed."

Georgie could tell Fanny wanted to say something further, but something in Zach's expression stopped her. Georgie herself felt sick to *her* stomach. The last thing on earth she wanted was to come between Zach and his daughter…or to cause them any more problems.

But she had.

She was the sole reason for Katie's stomachache.

I knew it was a mistake to go skating with Zach and the kids. Why hadn't she listened to herself? If she had, none of this would ever have happened.

I can't stay here.

In fact, I can't stay in New York. And the sooner I get out of both places, the better off everyone will be.

Chapter Twelve

Georgie could tell Zach was trying hard, but dinner was a strained affair. Even the children must have sensed that something was wrong, because they were more subdued than they'd been all day. Or maybe they were just tired. Georgie figured she didn't know them well enough to tell the difference.

Gamely, she tried to keep up her end of the conversation, and she managed well enough, although she could see Zach's mind was elsewhere. It didn't take a brain surgeon to figure out where, either. Knowing the kind of father Zach was, Georgie was sure he was worrying about Katie. Shoot, *she* was worrying about Katie.

Poor kid. She must have felt as if her world were spinning out of control. Georgie remembered how she'd felt when, after her dad died, her mother had gone to work.

Georgie had hated that. She was used to coming

home from school and Cornelia being there—a snack already made and waiting—some days fresh brownies, some days homemade peanut-butter cookies and always a bowl of fresh fruit. Georgie still remembered what a treat the first Rainier cherries had been, how she and her sisters would gorge themselves on them.

But then George Fairchild died, and everything changed. They'd had to move, there'd been a lot less money, and Cornelia had taken a job. It had been hard on all of them.

How would Georgie and her sisters have felt if they'd suspected their mother was getting interested in some other man while they were still mourning their father? Georgie had a feeling she'd have been just as appalled as Katie seemed to be.

Kids needed the security of a safe world, especially after the death of a beloved parent or a traumatic divorce. And that feeling of safety sure didn't include some other person stepping into the shoes of the missing parent.

No wonder Katie had behaved the way she had earlier. And no wonder Zach couldn't shake off what had happened as unimportant. If he had, Georgie would have thought a whole lot less of him.

Even little Emma was affected by tonight's mood. She was sitting to Zach's left, and every once in a while she would reach over and pat his hand. It was one of the sweetest things Georgie had ever seen, and the second time she did it—looking at Zach with those big, blue eyes of hers—Georgie had to fight to keep tears out of her eyes.

What am I doing here? I don't belong here. I'm just causing trouble.

If there were any possible way Georgie could have

climbed out of the wheelchair and walked out and left Zach and his children in peace, she would have.

By the time they were in the middle of their dessert—a delicious lemon pie that Georgie could see was homemade—Georgie was a wreck and she had a headache from thinking and worrying. She had also made a decision. She would spend tonight at Zach's apartment because she really had no other option except to move to a hotel, and she knew Zach would be even more upset if she did that. But tomorrow morning, as soon as she knew her mother would be awake, she planned to call Cornelia and ask her to come to New York to stay with her until she could function on her own.

The second call she'd make would be to Alex. She'd ask him to find someone else to help Zach until he could replace his assistant.

And then I'll go back to Seattle, where I belong.

Zach had planned for Georgie to remain at the apartment on Monday. He'd figured Fanny could pamper her, and Georgie could just rest her ankle by keeping her foot propped up while she read or watched television or napped. But Georgie wouldn't hear of it.

"I'm going to the office," she said firmly. "I'm all ready."

And she was. In fact, she'd been ready and waiting when he came back from seeing Katie and Jeremy off to school. Dressed in a dark skirt and white blouse, Georgie, along with Emma, was eating pancakes and bacon in the kitchen. When Zach walked in, Fanny was in the process of preparing another plate for him.

Zach felt better this morning, although he'd had a restless and worried night. He was still worried because he had no idea what to do about Katie other than to talk to her counselor and ask her to spend some extra time with his daughter. He guessed he should call Celeste Fouchet this morning, see if she could fit Katie in today.

What he wouldn't do was ask Georgie to leave the apartment, even though that's what Katie wanted. In fact, she'd turned stony when he told her he couldn't do that. After that, she'd refused to talk to him and she'd refused to come out for dinner. Her last gesture spoke volumes. When he'd left her room, she'd locked the door behind him.

All the rooms in his apartment had been fitted with locks as a safety measure. Zach had a master key. In fact, there were several. Fanny had one, too. The last thing he wanted was for one of his children—or anyone—to be trapped in a room accidentally.

So Katie locking the door was symbolic only, because she knew Zach could get in if he wanted to. It had hurt him to hear that click. He knew in her ten-year-old mind, she was locking him out of her heart, just as she thought he was locking her out of his.

All night last night, he'd been unable to forget the look of betrayal in her eyes while he'd tried to talk to her. He knew he'd let her down, yet he'd felt powerless to do anything else. He *couldn't* ask Georgie to leave. That wouldn't be right, and it wouldn't help Katie with the deeper problem of her inability to come to terms with Jenny's death.

You don't want Georgie to leave because you like having her close by. You like pretending she's something she's never going to be.

He had tried again this morning to get Katie to talk to him, but other than saying, "I'll be late for school, Dad," she had hardly even looked at him. He knew he couldn't let this situation go on. Whether or not she was hurting, she had to understand that she couldn't be rude to people, especially someone who was a guest in their home. He sighed inwardly. He wasn't looking forward to telling Katie she would have to apologize to Georgie.

"Mr. Prince," Fanny said, forcing him to stop thinking about last night and Katie's meltdown, "did you want me to call the cleaner today?" She set his breakfast on the table.

Zach nodded. "Thanks, Fanny. Make sure you tell them about that spot on my gray suit." Then, in an effort to lighten the atmosphere, he said to Emma, "Guess what? Nana is going to come and visit us next week."

"Nana!" Emma shouted. She was so excited that she knocked her fork on the floor and almost succeeded in sending her glass of milk right after it.

Zach pushed the glass out of the danger zone. "Be careful, honey."

"I want a doll this time!" Emma said, the volume of her voice still in high-decibel range.

"Jenny's mother always brings something for the kids when she visits," Zach said, feeling the need to explain to Georgie that there was a legitimate reason for Emma's expectation.

"My grandmother always had something for me and my sisters when she visited, too," Georgie said. She smiled, but it seemed halfhearted to Zach, as if her mind were elsewhere.

He hoped she didn't feel unwelcome, but with the way Katie had acted last night, he wouldn't blame Georgie if she did. He wished he could think of something to say to make her feel better, but he was at a loss right now. The best he could do was, "We'd better be going. I've got an interview set up for ten-thirty." The wall clock showed it was already after nine. He ignored the uneaten portion of his breakfast. Food was unappealing right now.

Fifteen minutes later he and Georgie sat in the back-seat of a cab inching its way through rush-hour traffic. The portable wheelchair had been folded up and was safely ensconced in the trunk, along with Georgie's crutches. Even though Zach had originally wanted Georgie to rest today, he had to admit he was glad now that she would be in the office today, and not just because he was afraid she would have been miserable at the apartment with only Fanny for company.

Truth was, he would miss her when she left for Seattle. In some ways, he was almost happy Luke Peterson had turned down the job. He smiled ruefully. If Alex knew how torn Zach felt, what would he say?

He'd say I need to get my hormones under control.

No. Alex wouldn't say that. Not Alex. Alex would understand, because he'd once confessed that the moment he met his wife, P.J., he hadn't had another second's peace. "Truth is," he'd said, "I fell like the proverbial ton of bricks."

That's what's happening to me. Trouble is, I can't do a damned thing about it, no matter how much I want to.

Sneaking a glance at Georgie, he caught her in an unguarded moment. Her face was turned away, but there was an undeniable air of tension about her, and he was seized by an almost uncontrollable urge to pull her into his arms. To tell her everything was going to be okay. *To tell her I…what? I don't have the right to tell her anything.*

Luckily, before he could do anything stupid, the moment passed, and the cab pulled up before their building.

Deborah jumped up from her desk to hold the door open when Zach and Georgie arrived. After maneuvering the wheelchair through, Zach and Deborah helped Georgie remove her coat. Then Deborah, who took the coat as well as Georgie's scarf and gloves, left Zach free to get Georgie settled in her office.

"You okay?" he asked once she was positioned behind her desk and Deborah had brought in a cup of coffee and the files Georgie needed to get started on the day's work.

"I'm fine, Zach. Thank you. I can manage on my own now."

There was no warmth in her voice, and she didn't meet his eyes. He wished he knew what she was thinking. She hadn't been this distant yesterday. Was there more bothering her than just Katie's behavior last night? Was Georgie finally feeling as if everything that had happened to her in the past two days were his fault? Was she regretting coming to New York at all?

He wanted to say how sorry he was. He wanted to say how much he cared for her. How much he wished he were free to see if what he had sensed between them were real. But how could he? What good would it do? He wasn't free. His kids had to take precedence over his needs. Katie needed him more than he needed Georgie.

Suddenly Zach felt as if his entire life were crashing down around him. He was only human. He could only do so much. And obviously, what he *was* doing was woefully inadequate in the eyes of everyone he loved.

That this was an exaggeration crossed his mind. Yet at that moment, it didn't feel that way. So he did what he had done in many moments of crisis.

He headed for his office to call his twin.

* * *

Georgie stared at Zach's closed door. She was so upset, her heart was pounding. She wasn't sure she could sit in this office today, even though she was the one who had insisted upon coming to work. But it would have been worse to sit in Zach's apartment all day long—an interloper, the woman who had caused Zach's troubled daughter such grief.

I have to get out of here just as soon as possible. I can't be around him. I've fallen in love with him. We've never even kissed, yet all I can think about is Zach. Nothing else seems important to me, and if I don't get away from him soon, I'm going to do something or say something I can't take back.

She bit her lip, looked at the clock. Almost ten, but still only seven in Seattle. Would her mother be awake yet?

I'll wait another half hour. When Zach's candidate shows up for his interview, I'll call her.

With any luck at all, her mother could be here tonight.

"Cornelia."

Cornelia had been staring out the tenth-floor window of the hospital. The lights of downtown Seattle and the more distant lights from various islands in Puget Sound were just beginning to fade as the morning sky brightened, but the vista, one she had always loved, didn't soothe her. For the past half hour, ever since Harry had been wheeled away, she'd been staring out sightlessly, lost in thought. Now, at the sound of Amelia's voice—Amelia was Gray's wife and a favorite of Cornelia's—she turned.

"Gray's going to walk over to Starbucks," Amelia said. "Would you like him to bring something back?"

Cornelia shook her head. "Thank you, dear. I don't want anything."

"Not even a cup of tea?"

"Not now. Thank you, anyway." Cornelia had spent the night at the hospital, even though Harry's sons and their wives all had urged her to go home and get some sleep. But she wouldn't. Couldn't. Somehow she felt if she kept her vigil, all would be well.

Harry was undergoing emergency bypass surgery that morning and was being prepped. The surgery was scheduled for eight o'clock. A blockage had been found and his cardiologist felt it was crucial to operate as soon as possible. Luckily, the heart surgeon that Dr. Kedar wanted was available. But knowing how people jumped when Harry needed or wanted them, Cornelia was certain the surgeon would have altered any previous plans to make sure he was free.

She'd debated calling her daughters last night but had decided to wait until this morning. There would be no point in having the girls rush to the hospital. It wasn't as if they could do anything to help. And they all led such busy lives and had so many commitments. Especially Frankie, with that restaurant of hers. It was enough that Harry's sons and their wives were here.

And me. I'll be here for as long as Harry wants me.

Cornelia didn't want to think that Harry might now have changed his mind about wanting to marry her, because the thought hurt. She wanted to believe he would still feel the exact same way, no matter the outcome of today's surgery. No matter his prognosis.

But maybe he wouldn't.

The thought made her long for the comfort of having her daughters close by. Because as much as she loved Harry's sons and their families, they weren't yet *hers*.

But it would be selfish to call the girls. She sighed, then brightened a bit. She could at least call Georgie. Georgie was thousands of miles away, so there was no danger she'd come barreling over to the hospital.

Cornelia rooted through her purse and pulled out her cell phone.

"Oh, Zach, I'm so glad you phoned," Sabrina said. "I've been sitting here hoping I'd hear from you this morning."

"This is the first chance I've had to call you."

"What happened with Katie last night?"

Zach sighed. "Not a helluva lot. Trouble is, she took an instant dislike to Georgie. She immediately saw Georgie as some kind of threat. I didn't tell you about it because…" Why *hadn't* he told Sabrina about that first encounter? "Because I was uncomfortable thinking it. I told myself she would have been upset to see me with another woman no matter who the woman was. I told myself she's just a child and she was imagining something that wasn't there."

It felt so good to unburden himself, Zach decided to be completely honest. "Truth is, Katie sensed something I hadn't even sensed myself." He then repeated that first conversation with Katie, how she'd asked if he was going to marry Georgie, how she'd wanted him to promise he wouldn't get married again.

"Oh, Zach," Sabrina said softly when he'd finished.

In those two words, Zach knew his sister understood everything.

"Tell me something, Zach," Sabrina said after a long moment of silence. "*Are* you in love with Georgie?"

"I don't know," he answered wearily. "I think I might be."

"If you were free—totally free—would you pursue a relationship with her?"

Again, in that uncanny way they often communicated without words, he knew Sabrina understood the doubts and guilt that plagued him, the way he now second-guessed everything he did and said when it came to his kids and their welfare and future.

Zach pictured Georgie, the way she probably looked right this minute, how vulnerable she seemed now that she was trapped in that wheelchair. He pictured the way she'd looked the day he met her. He thought about her confidence, her intelligence, her quick laughter, her sense of humor. He thought about the way she related to Jeremy and Emma, how they had already bonded with her. He thought about how kind she was, how much she cared about the work they did, the people they helped. "Yes," he said, " I'd pursue her." He'd grab onto her and not let go.

"So you *have* fallen in love with her."

"But Sabrina, don't you think that's crazy? I've only known Georgie *two weeks!* I haven't so much as kissed the woman."

"So? I knew Peter was the one for me the moment I met him. Love doesn't know rules, Zach. Love doesn't say you have to date a person X number of times or kiss them X number of times or anything else. Better minds than ours have tried to explain it. But the bottom line is, love is just…love."

Georgie jumped when her intercom buzzed.

"Georgie, your mother's on the line," Deborah said.

Was her mother a mind reader? Georgie wondered as she punched the extension. "Hi, Mom. I was just trying to decide if it was too early to call you." She forced her voice to sound upbeat.

"Hi, honey."

Her mother's voice sounded tired. Georgie frowned. Her mother was a morning person—always cheerful and eager to face the day. "Are you okay? You're not sick, are you?"

"No, I'm not sick."

"Then what is it? I can tell something's wrong."

"I have some bad news."

Georgie swallowed. "What?"

"It's Harry. He…he's had another heart attack, and this time they found a serious blockage. He's having bypass surgery right now."

"Oh, Mom. But he'll be all right, won't he?"

"I don't know. I hope so. We all hope so."

"Where are you? Are you at the hospital?"

"Yes."

"You're not alone there, are you?"

"No, of course not. All the boys are here…and their wives."

Georgie almost smiled at "the boys." She guessed Alex and his brothers would be "the boys" to her mother even when they were in their fifties and sixties, just as she and her sisters would always be "the girls."

"Are you okay?" Georgie asked gently.

"I'm doing all right. I—I just wanted to talk to one of my girls."

"You mean you haven't talked to any of the others?"

"No, I don't want them to feel they have to come running over here. They're all so busy, Georgie, you know that."

They talked for several more minutes, with Georgie reassuring her mother that Harry would be fine and getting her to promise she would call back the moment he was out of surgery and they knew anything more.

"I love you, Mom," Georgie said then. "Try not to worry. I'm sure he has the best doctors in Seattle and he'll be fine. Uncle Harry's tough. Remember that."

It was only after the call was over and her mother was no longer on the line that Georgie allowed herself to think of what her mother's call meant to her own situation.

Her mother could not come to New York.

Georgie would have to cope on her own.

And she could see no good way to get out of staying at Zach's apartment until she was mobile again.

Chapter Thirteen

Trying not to think about Georgie and how she'd barely spoken to him since they'd left the apartment that morning, Zach placed his call to Katie's counselor as soon as his interview was over. A minute later he had Celeste Fouchet on the phone.

"Has Katie tried to see you this morning?" he asked.

"No, why? Did something happen?"

"I'm afraid so." He went on to explain yesterday's drama and his subsequent attempts to talk to Katie. "I don't know what to do," he admitted. "I feel I shouldn't allow her to behave the way she did last night, no matter what prompted it. It's not acceptable to be rude to guests in our home. Is that expectation unreasonable?"

"No, Mr. Prince, it's not unreasonable," the counselor said. "I agree with you. However, we both know how frightened Katie must be. She obviously views this coworker of yours as a threat of some kind."

Zach sighed heavily. "I know. The first time she met Miss Fairchild, she asked me if I was going to marry her."

"I see. Are her feelings justified?"

Zach didn't resent the question or feel the counselor was out of line to ask it. He'd told her in the beginning, when she'd first begun working with Katie, that she could feel free to ask him anything that might help her determine how best to help his daughter. "Let's put it this way," he said quietly. "If I didn't have Katie's emotional welfare to worry about, I would be more than a little interested in a relationship with Miss Fairchild. And Katie obviously sensed that."

The counselor was silent for a long moment. When she spoke again, her voice was thoughtful. "I'll send for Katie after her lunch period is over. See if she'll open up to me. I'll get back to you later this afternoon, but I know you understand that, with very few exceptions, I can't divulge anything she's said to me in confidence."

Zach felt better when they'd hung up. Having someone he could turn to, someone who was trained to work with troubled kids, was a huge relief. Because no matter how much he loved Katie and wanted to help her return to the secure and happy child she'd once been, he was always afraid he would do or say the wrong thing and undermine the progress she'd already made.

Getting up, he opened his door. And just as he did, Georgie's door opened across the hall. She seemed startled to see him standing there. And he was startled to see her using her crutches.

"Do you need help?" he said. "Can I get you anything?"

"No, I'm fine."

"Does your ankle hurt? Maybe you should stay in the wheelchair today."

"I said I'm fine, Zach."

He flinched at the edge to her voice. He couldn't seem to do a thing right today.

By now, Deborah had walked out into the hall, too. She'd probably heard the clump of the crutches on the tile floor. "Where are you going, Georgie?"

Georgie's face was stony. "I'm going to the bathroom." Then, before Deborah or Zach could say anything else, she said, "I have to get used to doing things myself. I can't stay at Zach's apartment indefinitely."

Zach knew nothing he said would erase the expression in her eyes, the one that told him she was almost as unhappy as his daughter. As both he and Deborah watched Georgie's awkward progress down the hall toward the restroom, Zach wondered how it was he had made both the daughter he loved and the woman he wished he had the right to love so miserable.

"Dad is doing well, but he's weak and groggy and can only communicate with grunts."

Again, the messenger was Gray, who had just come from the recovery room where Harry would be kept until they could safely remove the tube in his throat. Cornelia had been on pins and needles as she waited to hear what Gray had to say. To minimize risk of infection, he had been the only one of Harry's sons allowed to go into the recovery room after the surgery was over. Harry's other boys and their wives had kept vigil with Cornelia in the waiting area.

Gray smiled at her. "I did tell him you were still here, and he lit up like a Christmas tree."

Cornelia bit her lip. Now that the surgery was successfully completed, she felt like crying. She knew the long hours of stress had finally caught up with her, and she fought what she considered weakness.

"I also asked him who he wanted to see first when he finally gets to go to his room, and without saying a word, he let me know it was you, Cornelia."

Cornelia could no longer hold back her tears. And when Harry's lovely boys and their beautiful wives surrounded her in a group hug, with lots of pats on the back, she finally felt that maybe, just maybe, everything might still turn out all right.

It was nearly five o'clock before Celeste Fouchet called Zach back. "I'm sorry, Mr. Prince, that it's taken so long to get back to you."

"Did you get a chance to talk to Katie?"

"Yes, I was able to switch another appointment and see Katie during her afternoon study period."

Zach knew the headmistress would have okayed Katie missing a class, if necessary, but he was glad that it hadn't been.

"At first, Katie didn't want to talk about what happened last night. In fact, she was upset that you'd called me."

Zach wasn't surprised.

"I told her that, as always, whatever she wanted to tell me would be confidential, between me and her, and that I would only tell you what she had given me permission to tell you."

"I realize that," Zach said.

"And what I can tell you is that you are correct in your assumptions about the root of Katie's antipathy toward your assistant. Katie's also given me permission to tell you that she knows she behaved badly, and she has promised me she will apologize to Miss Fairchild this evening."

Zach guessed he shouldn't have hoped for more. Yet he had. "After talking to Katie, do you have any advice for me?"

"Actually, I do. Despite behavior to the contrary, Katie shows signs that she's almost ready to move on. I think she's really tired of being sad all the time, but she hasn't known how to let go of that sadness. I think it's actually quite healthy that she's now showing some anger and acting out instead of keeping everything bottled up inside. That tells me if you're patient a little while longer, she just might surprise you."

Georgie wasn't sure she'd be able to manage another evening of chaotic emotions bubbling under the surface. So when Zach suggested she might like to rest awhile before dinner, she leaped at the suggestion. She even managed to smile at him.

"I'll ask Fanny to bring you some ice for your ankle," he said.

He really was such a good guy. She felt ashamed that she'd snapped at him today. Her only excuse was that she wasn't herself right now, and her ankle *was* hurting. In fact, it was killing her. Not only would she ice it, but she would take a couple of the pain pills the doctor had given her. If she were lucky, she thought ruefully, maybe she'd fall asleep and not wake up till it was time for her to go home.

She had just taken off her shoes and put a pillow under her ankle when there was a knock at the door. "Yes?" she called.

The door opened a crack, and Katie stuck her head around. "Miss...Fairchild?"

"Hello, Katie."

"M-may I come in?"

Georgie's voice softened. The child was scared. "Of course, honey."

Katie entered and closed the door behind her.

Georgie tried not to look surprised.

"I wanted to talk to you," Katie said. She still hadn't met Georgie's eyes. "I—I wanted to apologize."

Georgie almost said, "For what?" but stopped herself just in time. "Thank you. I accept your apology."

Katie looked down, toed one ballet-flat-clad foot.

Georgie's heart twisted. She wished she had the right to fold Katie in her arms and tell her she would never do anything to hurt her. "Katie," she said softly, "I know how you feel."

Katie's head jerked up, and her dark eyes flashed. "You *don't* know how I feel."

"Maybe not exactly, but my father died when I was twelve." Without warning, a lump formed in Georgie's throat.

Katie stared at her. "He did?" she finally said.

Georgie nodded. "Yes. So I can at least guess how you might feel. At least, I know how sad and scared I felt at the time."

Katie didn't answer. Instead, she walked over to the window and looked out. Georgie waited. She'd worked with kids enough to know they would talk to you on their terms. You couldn't force them. She was glad for the moment of reprieve, anyway. It allowed her to get hold of her emotions.

"I don't want my dad to get married again," Katie said, still without turning away from the window.

"I know."

Katie finally looked at her again. She seemed to consider, then blurted out, "Did your mom get married again?"

Georgie shook her head. "No. But after a while I wanted her to."

Katie's gaze was unblinking.

Georgie knew the child didn't believe her. "I wanted a dad so badly. My mom was great, but I wanted a dad to come to my soccer games and take me out sailing like my best friend's dad did."

"I—I want my mom to go shopping with me like Meredith's mom does."

Oh, honey, I wish I could take you shopping. But what I wish more is that I could take the hurt away. "I did have an uncle that I loved, though," Georgie said, keeping her voice matter-of-fact. "He was kind of like a dad, except he wasn't there all the time, like a dad is. I missed that. A lot." Georgie figured that explaining Harry's actual relationship to their family wasn't necessary. "That best friend I told you about? Her dad was really cool, and sometimes…I'd pretend he was *my* dad." Georgie hadn't thought about that in a long time, much less admitted it to anyone.

Katie swallowed. "I have an aunt."

"Yes, I know, your aunt Sabrina."

Katie nodded, looked away again.

Georgie's heart felt sore. Zach's daughter looked so vulnerable, so raw. If only Georgie could think of what to say to help her.

After a long, long moment, Katie turned back to Georgie. Her eyes were desolate. "Why do people have to die?" she whispered, her bottom lip trembling. "Moms shouldn't die."

Georgie felt her eyes filling. She didn't try to stop them. This was the time for honesty. "All of us have to die sometime, honey. I know your mom didn't want to leave you, but she couldn't help it. She was sick."

Katie nodded again. "That's what everybody says."

"It doesn't help, does it?"

Katie shook her head. Another long moment passed, during which the only sounds were of the traffic below and a clock chiming the hour from somewhere in the apartment. When Katie met Georgie's gaze again, she was more composed, her mask once again in place. "I'm sorry your ankle got hurt."

"Thank you." Georgie wasn't sure if they'd passed some kind of milestone or not. The child was too accustomed to covering up her emotions.

"But I still don't want my dad to get married again."

Georgie's heart ached as she watched Katie walk out of the room.

It was nine o'clock Monday evening before Harry's doctors pronounced him ready for short visits with his family. But only one at a time. When Dr. Kedar gave them the go-ahead, he added that Harry wished to see Cornelia first.

Earlier in the day, Cornelia had been persuaded to allow Walter to take her home briefly so that she could shower and change into fresh clothes, so at least she felt she looked as good as she could when she walked into Harry's private alcove in the CCU.

Her heart skipped when she got her first glimpse of him. Harry, big, strong, powerful Harry, looked so out of place in the hospital bed, with all those beeping machines and tubes and wires. But his dark eyes, which nothing seemed to dim, gleamed at her as she approached.

"Cornelia, there you are," he said, his voice raspy and weaker than she'd ever heard it.

She imagined his throat hurt from that breathing tube they'd inserted during the bypass surgery. "Hello, Harry." She grasped his left hand and bent over to kiss his cheek. He smelled like hospital.

He squeezed her hand. "Always so beautiful."

Cornelia shook her head. "And, as always, you're full of baloney."

He grinned, and in that moment, looked like the Harry of old. "What I'm full of is drugs."

She smiled. "Are you in pain?"

"Not right this minute. But if I try to move, or cough, it'll be like somebody stickin' knives in me." His expression became serious. "I'm sorry about all this, Corny."

"Sorry about what? That you had another heart attack? It wasn't your fault."

"We both know if I'd led a different kind of life, with less stress and all, I would've been a lot healthier today."

"We could all say that, couldn't we? The truth is, we've all made mistakes. But the thing about mistakes is, we learn from them."

He looked away. "Yes," he said sadly.

Cornelia frowned. "What's wrong? You're not worried, are you? Dr. Lessing says everything went extremely well, and Dr. Kedar says now that they've fixed this problem, if you behave yourself, you'll be in tip-top shape."

Still he didn't look at her.

"Harry, what is it?" Alarm caused her voice to sound

too loud in the small room, and she lowered it. "Please tell me what's wrong."

He finally turned his gaze back to her, and the sadness and regret in his eyes made her heart start beating too fast. "I just wish things could have turned out differently for us, dear heart."

"Wh-what do you mean?"

"I'm sorrier than you'll ever know, Cornelia," he managed, his voice getting weaker by the second, "but much as I still love you, I no longer feel we have a future together."

Cornelia was actually halfway back to the waiting area before the shock of Harry's announcement gave way to disbelief and then to indignation. Finally, a spurt of red-hot anger propelled her right back to his alcove.

"Harry Hunt," she said, glaring at him, "I don't care how sick you are right now. You take that back. You are *not,* repeat *not,* going to walk away from me again. I refuse to let you. I want that ring you promised *me* and I want us to be married, and it's me who won't take no for an answer this time."

Harry, whose eyes had been closed, looked stunned, but only for a moment. Then, a big smile wreathing his face, he sputtered, "When did you get so bossy?"

A moment later, heedless of the tubes and bottles and beeping machines, Cornelia was kissing his lips, although she was careful not to put even an ounce of weight on his poor, sore chest. Oh, she loved him, this big old idiot of a man. And the fact that he'd tried to free her because of his heart problems—which she knew without him having to tell her—only made her love him more.

She left him then, so his sons and daughters-in-law

could have their few minutes before they all got chased out of the CCU. But her heart was singing, because the last thing he said to her before she walked out was, "Pick our wedding day, Corny. Just make it soon."

Zach couldn't sleep. He wished he knew what Katie and Georgie had talked about so long, but neither his daughter nor the woman he was obsessed with seemed inclined to tell him anything. He'd tried to talk to Katie, who'd politely said she had homework to do. After Katie had gone off to her room and bed, and he'd said good-night to Jeremy and Emma and seen them tucked in, he'd gone back to the family room to find Georgie.

But she was no longer there. And when he'd gone looking for her, thinking maybe she'd wheeled herself out to the kitchen, the only person he'd found was Fanny, who'd just fixed herself a cup of tea and was carrying it toward her own suite.

"Georgie around?" he'd said.

"She went to her room, Mr. Price. Said she had a headache and was going to go to bed."

Zach had tried not to show how disappointed he was or how defeated he felt. The small burst of optimism he'd experienced when Katie's counselor had said she felt if he were just patient a little while longer, Katie might surprise him, had faded. Would he even *have* a little while longer? Georgie would be gone soon, and whatever chance he might have had with her would be gone with her.

All these thoughts, and more, tumbled through his mind as he tossed and turned in his king-size bed. Finally, close to two o'clock, he got up, grabbed a robe, stuffed his feet into slippers and very quietly opened his bedroom door and headed toward the kitchen. He would get a glass of milk and maybe a slice of that chocolate cake Fanny had baked earlier today.

The apartment, because of its top-quality workmanship and superior insulation, plus the double-paned windows Zach had had installed years earlier to cut noise and the effects of weather extremes, was silent except for the faint sounds of nighttime traffic in Manhattan.

As Zach rounded the corner into the kitchen, he stopped dead. For standing in front of the open refrigerator, bracing herself on the door, was Georgie. She hadn't heard him or seen him, because her back was to the doorway. Nowhere did he see the wheelchair...or the crutches. Had she walked on that ankle of hers? No, wait a minute. He spied one crutch. It was lying across two of the chairs, partially hidden by the table.

He watched her for a minute, his heart beating hard. Her hair tumbled loosely down her back, and even though she wore some kind of knit pajamas, the light from the refrigerator shined through the soft material to reveal the outline of her long, sleek body. The side of one perfect breast was visible in silhouette, and Zach's body reacted immediately.

He wanted this woman. He wanted her badly. But if he were smart, he'd turn around before she knew he was there and go back to his room and stay there.

However, his brain wasn't the dominant organ just then, and before he could stop himself, he whispered, "Georgie."

She startled and lost her balance.

Zach lunged toward her and grabbed her from behind, pulling her close and holding her steady. She was breathing hard, as if she'd run a race. Burying his head in her hair, he closed his eyes, tried to get his raging desire under control. Her hair smelled of vanilla and cinnamon and something else, something uniquely Georgie.

She didn't move.

And then, slowly, still holding her securely, he turned her in his arms. Now they were standing body to body, and as if it were someone else controlling him, he drew her closer still, until he could feel the length of her legs against his, the swell of her hips, the warmth of her belly, the curve of her breasts. His erection strained against his pajama bottoms, and he didn't even care. Nothing mattered at that moment except the rightness of the woman in his arms.

When he dipped his head—not far, she was nearly as tall as he was—and captured her mouth with his, she sighed deeply and twined her arms around him.

Georgie. The thought pounded through him, right along with the blood that coursed through his veins and the desire that exploded in its wake. The kiss went on and on, became two, then three, a feast for two starving people.

It was only when the clock on the mantel in the dining room struck the hour that reality struck them.

Georgie was the first to push away. Breathing hard, she said, "Please hand me my crutch."

Silently, he reached for it and gave it to her. His heart was still pounding. Every part of him ached. He wanted her. He needed her. He knew what he'd done was crazy. Especially here. In his apartment, with his children sleeping close by. With Fanny sleeping close by.

"I'm sorry," he said. "I shouldn't have—"

"I'm going home tomorrow," Georgie said, cutting

him off. She didn't look at him. "I can't stay here another day."

And then, slowly, awkwardly—managing somehow not to make any noise—she turned and walked out of the room.

Chapter Fourteen

"Zach?"

Zach looked up from his desk. Deborah stood in his open doorway.

"I just got a call from Tommy's school," she said. "He's running a fever and they want me to come and get him. I'd ask Jack to go, but he's tied up in a meeting in Boston today. I'm really sorry. I know today's a bad day for this."

Zach suppressed a sigh. He didn't want Deborah to feel guilty because her son took precedence over a work overload here. He'd rushed home several times to be with a sick child. "You go on. Don't worry about anything. I hope Tommy's okay."

Deborah gave him a worried nod, poked her nose in Georgie's office for a minute to say goodbye, then quickly left.

Zach eyed Georgie's partially closed door. It was

Thursday morning, and ever since the wee hours of Tuesday morning, when they'd kissed in the kitchen, she'd stayed away from him as much as possible. She'd gone back to the corporate apartment Tuesday after work, and she'd refused his help in getting there. She'd also refused to take the wheelchair, saying she needed to use the crutches because they gave her more freedom.

Zach got up and walked to the windows overlooking Eighth Avenue. He was surprised to see it was snowing. This snow looked wet, more like freezing rain, and he could tell, even from up here, that the wind was blowing hard. He hoped Deborah didn't have a problem collecting Tommy and getting home.

If conditions didn't improve after lunch, he should close down the office early. Once again, he looked around at Georgie's office door. He could hear faint tapping, which meant she was working at her keyboard. That almost-closed door seemed to symbolize everything that had happened—or not happened—between them. At least she hadn't shut it completely. Did that mean something, too?

He was sorry she was so obviously upset over what had happened between them. He wasn't—despite the fact that he couldn't see a way around their myriad problems. If nothing else, at least he'd held Georgie in his arms. But most important, he'd confirmed that what he felt for her was real.

Now all he had to do was figure out what he could do about it.

Georgie heard Deborah leave. She also heard Zach moving around in his office. She forced herself to keep working. *Stay focused. Don't think. And especially don't think about those kisses and the way they made you feel.*

But that was like telling herself not to breathe, because those kisses, and Zach, were all Georgie had been able to think about for two days now. Two and a half days, to be precise.

Georgie's eyes swam with tears, which made her so mad at herself that she wanted to throw something. The only good thing about her life right now was her mother's happiness, and that was pretty sad.

Her mother was walking on air right now. She'd called Georgie Tuesday to tell her that Harry was going to be fine and that they were officially engaged.

"Oh, Georgie," she'd said, "wait until you see my ring. It's so big it'll knock your eyes out. And everyone else's, too!"

Georgie actually smiled, thinking about that conversation. It was hard not to be happy for her mother. Even though Georgie's own love life was in Hopeless City.

And then, of course, there were her sisters, all of whom were either happily married or happily engaged. If only Chick would dump Joanna, then Georgie would have someone to commiserate with her. Georgie didn't *really* want Joanna to be unhappy just because *she* was, but still…it was hard to be the only woman in the universe without someone to cuddle with at night. She might have to get a dog.

On and on her thoughts went. Finally, disgusted with herself, she opened her drawer, took out her iPod, popped in the earbuds, chose her hard-rock playlist and turned the volume up loud.

Maybe she could blast away the voice in her head.

At four o'clock, Zach considered closing the office because the weather was rapidly worsening. But he saw traffic moving below, including a lot of cabs, so he knew

Georgie could get home okay, and that was the only thing that worried him. She still couldn't put her full weight on that ankle of hers and needed her crutches. He, of course, could walk home, no problem. It was only about ten blocks.

Unfortunately, he couldn't leave, because he was expecting a phone call from the governor, who only had the office number. Zach had called Fanny earlier to alert her to the fact that he might be late coming home tonight.

Georgie didn't have to stick around, though. Taking a deep breath, he crossed the hall, rapped lightly, then pushed her door open. Georgie, who'd been facing her computer, turned abruptly, as if he'd startled her.

"The weather's getting worse. I think you should go home." His conscience pricked him about how tired she looked. Was that his doing? Maybe she wasn't sleeping well, either.

"I'm fine, Zach. In fact, I was planning to stay until six or even later." She gestured to the stacks of files on her desk. "There's a lot to do." Her eyes, green enigmatic pools, met his again. "I'm also going to take work home this weekend."

"You don't have to do that."

"I want to get through as much of this backlog as possible, because I really need to get back to Seattle as soon as I can."

"Georgie…" he said softly.

"I'd like to leave by the end of next week." Her tone was perfectly polite, but it said, *Don't argue with me.*

"Look, can we please talk about the other ni—" But before he could finish, two things happened. She started to shake her head, and all the lights went out. Because there were no windows in her office, the only light—and it wasn't much—filtered over from his office.

"What happened?" she said.

"I don't know. Either the building lost power or our floor lost power. I'm not sure how the electricity is set up. We've been here three years and have never had a problem before. Don't move. I'll go across to my office, where I'll be able to see a little better and call downstairs."

Five minutes later, after a conversation with the security guard—unfortunately a new man who didn't have a clue about the electricity setup and who said the maintenance department had closed at noon because the supervisor had a funeral to go to—Zach realized they might be stuck without electricity for a while.

It wasn't until he'd looked outside that he discovered all the buildings in his line of sight were also dark. His heart sank. It wasn't just their building—something had happened to the entire grid they were in. And for all he knew, the entire city.

The sky was already dark because of the weather. Swearing under his breath, he walked to his open doorway. "Georgie." He could just make her out now that his eyes had adjusted to the lack of light. "Stay put. I don't want you falling. I'm going to go into the kitchenette and find the flashlight, and I think we have some candles in there."

Five minutes later he'd found two votive candles, matches and a flashlight and had gone back to his office and lit the candles, then—flashlight in hand—walked back across to Georgie's office.

"C'mon," he said, going behind her desk to help her with her crutches. "Let's get you into my office where you'll be more comfortable. You can sit on the couch and prop your ankle on the coffee table."

"But Zach, what's the point? Why don't we just go home? It's not like we'll get any work done now."

"Yeah, I know. I thought of that while I was in the kitchen."

"Then why…?"

"The trouble is, we're on the eighteenth floor. And if the power is out, the elevators are not working."

It took a moment for the import of his statement to sink in. "Oh."

"Yes. Oh."

They both knew she could not walk down eighteen flights of stairs. One or two, probably. Half a dozen, maybe. Eighteen flights, no way.

And much as he would like to, he couldn't carry her. Even supporting her would be problematic, because he already suspected the reason she was still using her crutches was that she'd rushed walking on her foot when she'd fled from his apartment and that had delayed its recovery.

They were stuck here for the duration.

Oh, dear heaven, Georgie thought.

Her heart was beating so hard she was sure Zach could feel it, for even though she was using her crutches, he had a firm hold on her. Even that touch, as casual as it was, had made her feel as if she might fall apart at any moment. The only way she'd been able to survive the past few days was to stay as far away from Zach physically as it was possible to be. She'd even kept her door at least partially closed the whole time she was in the office, because otherwise she'd have been too tempted to look across the hall. She had to stay strong; otherwise she was doomed.

With the help of the flashlight, Zach managed to guide her across the hall and into his office without mishap. He settled her onto the couch, put one of the decorative throw pillows behind her back and the other on top of the coffee table, where she propped the still-slightly-swollen ankle.

"I've got to make some phone calls," he said. "Do you want me to get you something to drink?"

"No, I'm fine, Zach. Don't worry about me." *I'll just sit here and enjoy being close to you without you being able to see how rattled I am.*

Over the next thirty minutes or so, Zach found out—and relayed to Georgie—that there was also no power at his apartment but that his children were all safely home. Fanny had said she'd been making a stew when the electricity went, but it was so close to being done that they could still have it for dinner.

"She told me not to worry," Zach added wryly.

He'd also discovered that just about everyone in their building had been able to get down the stairs and out of the building except for one older wheelchair-bound man from the tenth floor. The security guard was on duty until midnight and told Zach he hoped the power would be restored long before then.

"Me, too," Georgie said, although down deep, she thought life might be perfect if she and Zach could just stay there forever, only the two of them. Their own little desert island. *Oh, Georgie, what a mess you are!*

After those two conversations, he tried getting hold of ConEd, but everyone in the city who had a working phone must have been calling them, because all Zach got was a busy signal or voice mail. After leaving two messages, Zach gave up.

While he was still on his last call—he was using his cell phone—the office phone rang. It would work, Zach told her, until the charge ran out. This call, Georgie surmised from the conversation, was his anticipated one from the governor's office. Georgie leaned her head back and closed her eyes while he talked. She liked listening to his voice. Actually, she liked every single thing about him. Even his children. If only Katie liked *her*.

Things might not be perfect if Katie's attitude toward Georgie was different, but at least then there'd be hope. Because right now this blackout or brownout, or whatever the heck it was, was the only hope Georgie had of ever again being alone with Zach.

Finally his call with the governor was over. "I can't think of anyone else to call," he said. "I'm afraid all we can do now is wait."

"Too bad we don't have a little TV that runs on batteries," Georgie said, but she didn't really want one there. She had everything she wanted right here in this office.

The candlelight cast shadows on his face, on the room, everywhere. Zach got up and stretched. He looked out the window again. "The only lights down there come from the cars. The streets must be a mess with the traffic lights out and freezing rain still falling."

"How do you know it's freezing?"

"It's sticking to the window." He turned to face her and leaned against the sill. "I'm really sorry about this, Georgie."

"It's not your fault. What I'm sorry about is that you're stuck here with me." She made a face. "If not for me, you'd be home by now."

"There's nobody I'd rather be stuck with than you."

This was said so softly that at first Georgie wasn't sure she'd heard correctly. When what he'd said sank in, she could feel her face heating. The good thing was, he couldn't tell she was blushing in the candlelight.

Her heart skittered as he walked over to the sofa and sat beside her, leaving only a couple of inches between them.

"I don't want you to leave next week, Georgie." His voice felt like velvet in her ears.

Georgie swallowed. Slowly, she turned her head so that she could look at him. There was just enough light in the room for her to see his expression, and what she saw made her stupid heart thunder like a triphammer. "I—I don't want to go, either."

"Then why are you?"

She sighed deeply and looked away. "You know I have to, Zach."

"Why? Because of what happened the other night?"

"Not just that," she whispered.

"Then what?"

"Please, Zach…"

"Look at me, Georgie."

"I…"

"Look at me."

When she turned back to him, he pulled her into his arms. And just before his lips claimed hers, he muttered, "You have no idea how much I want you."

Her last rational thought was, *Yes, I do, because I want you the same way.*

Afterward, she never remembered him removing her sweater or helping her take off the rest of her clothes or him shucking his with her help. What she did remember was how right his skin felt next to hers, and how perfectly their bodies fit each other.

The couch wasn't long enough for them, but it didn't seem to matter. Nothing mattered to Georgie but this man and this moment. It was as if they were inhabitants of another world: a world of soft candlelight and warm flesh, a world of shadows and wildly beating hearts, a world of undiscovered pleasure and untold passions.

Their first kisses were greedy, as if they couldn't get enough of each other, as if they knew deep inside that this would be their only chance to seize what they both so desperately wanted.

Zach was a wonderful lover. He seemed to know instinctively just where to touch her, just where to place his lips, his tongue, his hands. When she moaned, he whispered, "Do you like that?"

"Oh, yes," she said. "Yes."

She loved hearing his swift intake of breath when she returned the favors, and hearing his response, she became bolder.

Several times he cried out, which made her bolder still.

Her skin felt on fire, and when he lifted her so that she was lying on top of him and she could feel the hard length of his body under hers, she opened her legs and guided him inside. She was wet and ready, and now it was her turn to gasp as he gripped her bottom with both hands and she felt him push deeper and deeper.

"Oh," she said. "Oh." Why had she not known it would be this way? How could she ever do without him now that she did know? She wanted to laugh out loud, to cry and shout. This…this was everything.

Fully inside her now, he began to move, slowly at first, in and out, and she moved with him. His hands on her bottom felt hot. She loved that. She could stay joined like this forever.

Her orgasm began quickly, too quickly. Yet she wouldn't have stopped it if she could, because her body was out of her control now. Her body was his, and he could do with it what he wanted.

She cried out as the first waves began, and he clasped her more firmly and drove faster and harder, so that her pleasure became even more intense. *Was there anything more wonderful than this?* she thought as the pleasure went on and on. Then, after one more mighty thrust, his body shuddered violently and she felt his life force erupt inside.

Zach. The thought was a prayer. A poem. Her only reality.

He finally stilled, and with their hearts still beating madly, he rolled her over and fit his body to hers, her back to his front. He held her close so she wouldn't fall off the sofa, one hand cupping her left breast, the other delving until it found the spot that still craved his touch. Gently, he stroked, and she could feel his smile against her cheek as her body arched once more.

"You're everything I thought you'd be, Georgie," he whispered. "Beautiful and passionate and perfect."

But she couldn't answer, for she was cresting once again.

Ten minutes later, the lights blazed on.

Georgie, whose eyes had been closed, jumped and would have fallen off the couch if he hadn't held on. Hurriedly, averting her gaze from his, she grabbed her clothes and put on her sweater. Her eyes kept darting to the window, and Zach knew she was embarrassed and afraid that someone could see in. He doubted it, but the faster they got dressed, the better, because he was afraid that new security guard would come up to check on them if they didn't hightail it down there quickly.

Georgie managed to get her skirt on, and still without looking at Zach she said, "I'm going into the restroom to dress."

And before he could help her gather up her things, she'd scooped up her undies, limped over to where her crutches were and hobbled out of the office.

"Dammit," he said. He got dressed quickly, not even caring if someone did see him. They wouldn't know who he was. Besides, he wasn't ashamed of what he and Georgie had done. He was proud. He was happy. He loved her, and now he knew she felt the same way, even though she hadn't said so. "Somehow we're going to work this out," he muttered.

After grabbing his cell phone, scarf and gloves, he walked out into the hall. Georgie was just coming out of the restroom.

"Can you get my coat and things for me?" she said.

"Sure." After retrieving them from her office, he helped her into her coat, his hand lingering against her cheek.

For one moment, she leaned into his hand. Then she straightened and said briskly, "We'd better go. Your family will expect you soon."

"Don't you think we need to talk?" Surely things had changed. Surely she wasn't going to go back to not speaking to him.

She sighed, turned to look at him. In her eyes he saw something that made him wary. "Zach," she said, her voice resigned. "There's really nothing to talk about, because nothing has changed."

"What do you mean? *Everything* has changed."

"Why? Just because we...had sex?"

He stiffened. "Is that what you think? That we just had sex?"

"Well, didn't we?"

"We made love, Georgie, and you know it."

She shook her head. "It doesn't matter what you call it. Nothing has changed. We're still from two different worlds. This is where you belong, Zach, and I don't. Just ask Katie. She'll tell you."

And for the second time in a week, she turned and walked away from him. But this time, she was taking his heart with her.

Chapter Fifteen

Ten days later ...

Zach knew the kids were looking at him. He also knew they were bewildered by his behavior. He wished they were old enough to understand his plight, because he was exhausted by the effort of trying to pretend nothing was wrong, and tonight he simply wasn't able to pretend anymore.

Earlier today he'd cried on Sabrina's shoulder. Not literally, of course. Grown men didn't cry, did they? They sucked it up. *Hang tough.* Wasn't that what his dad always said? Sabrina could cry. Zach had to hang tough.

"Dad?" Jeremy said. "Wanna watch *Shrek 2* with us?"

"I don't think so, Jeremy. You guys go on, though."

Out of the corner of his eye, he saw Katie frown.

"I wanna watch *Cinderella,*" Emma said, already beginning to pout.

"You always want to watch *Cinderella,*" Jeremy said. He kicked the leg of the chair where Emma was sitting and stuck out his tongue. "I'm watching *Shrek 2!*"

"Daddy!" Emma shouted.

"Jeremy, stop that," Zach said. He couldn't even muster up enough energy to make it sound like he meant it. Ignoring Jeremy's cries of "You always yell at me and not her. I hate her," he left the kids to settle their squabble by themselves and headed into the kitchen, where he opened the refrigerator and stared inside.

"Mr. Prince?"

Zach turned to see Fanny standing in the doorway.

"Can I get you something?" she asked.

'Thanks, Fanny. I'm not really hungry." He shut the door and, feeling like a fool, said, "I'm going into my study for a while. Will you keep an eye on those kids?" He could still hear Jeremy and Emma arguing.

"Of course."

She didn't add, "Don't I always?" but Zach knew that that's what she was thinking. She was probably also thinking he was crazy. Well, maybe he was. Ever since Georgie left for Seattle the day after the brownout, he'd felt as if his world had once again fallen apart.

Why? Why had she gone? Why had she given herself to him so freely, so joyfully even, then disappeared from his life as if she'd never been there at all? She hadn't even called him to say goodbye, just sent a text saying she was sorry, but she was going home.

For the hundredth time, maybe the thousandth time, he told himself that there wasn't anything else he could have done to stop her. Georgie had been right about one thing: His life was here, in this apartment, in this city, with his children. Even if Katie should miraculously come around and be fine with him marrying again, his life would still be here. He was committed. And he guessed, from what Georgie said, that she couldn't see herself sharing that commitment.

She doesn't love you. Get over it.

But could he? That was the big question. Could he?

Would she ever forget him?

Would she ever see a tall, dark-haired man and not immediately think of Zach? Would she ever see deep blue eyes or a gorgeous smile and not feel as if someone had knocked the air out of her?

She stared out of the front window of her condo. It was raining, the soft, light rain that was so common to Seattle in March. Soon the flowers would be in bloom, but Georgie doubted she'd be here to see them. Alex had promised her a new assignment in the field, and she expected to be leaving soon. Even that didn't excite her much, certainly not the way it would have in the past.

She'd been back home now for more than a week, and nothing excited her, nothing made her happy. She couldn't sleep. She had no interest in eating. She'd lost eight pounds she didn't need to lose. Even gazing at her beloved Puget Sound didn't soothe her the way it always had.

Why? she thought. *Why did I have to fall in love with a man I can't have? And what am I going to do now?*

"I'm worried about Georgie," Cornelia told Harry. "She seems so unhappy, but when I ask her what's wrong, she says 'nothing.'"

Harry shrugged. "Maybe it's her time of the month."

"Oh, Harry, for heaven's sake. I thought you were

smarter than that!" Cornelia didn't want to laugh, but she couldn't help it, so she punched his arm in retaliation for the clueless remark.

"What did I say?" He rubbed his arm as if she'd actually hurt him, which she knew she hadn't, because the so-called punch had been a love tap. "Corny, you know I don't understand anything about women. Aren't you always telling me that? I didn't have daughters, I had sons."

"I know," she said, sighing. "I'm just frustrated, because I know what's wrong with Georgie. I just don't know how to help her."

"Well if you know, will you please tell me?"

Cornelia rolled her eyes. "She's in love, and something went wrong." When Harry stared at her, she decided she should confess what she'd known since their trip to New York.

"Well, I'll be darned," Harry said when she'd finished. "Zach Prince. And I didn't suspect a thing."

"I guess you're not such a great matchmaker, after all," Cornelia said, laughing again. She seemed to laugh a lot nowadays.

"You talk too much," Harry said, reaching for her. "But I know how to stop you."

After that, they didn't talk at all.

"Dad, can I talk to you?"

Zach looked up from his laptop. Katie stood in the doorway of the study. He forced himself to sound enthusiastic, even though he didn't feel like talking to anyone. "Sure, honey. Come on in." He knew she was still waiting on an answer about riding lessons, because she'd mentioned it again yesterday. Oh, hell. He'd let her take lessons. At least *she'd* be happy then.

Giving him a hesitant smile, Katie sat in one of two leather chairs in the room.

Zach's heart caught as he really looked at his daughter, maybe for the first time in weeks. She was fast approaching her eleventh birthday, and she was changing. Right now she looked more like her mother than ever before. Katie would be a beautiful woman someday.

"Dad," she said again, then stopped and seemed to be searching for how to say what she wanted.

"Let me make it easy for you," he said, smiling at her, his first genuine smile in days. "I've decided you can take riding lessons."

"That...that would be great, Dad, but that's not what I wanted to talk to you about. I—I wanted to ask you—" she swallowed "—why you're so sad all the time."

"I'm not sad—" Zach stopped. *Don't lie to her.* "It's complicated, honey. It...it's a grownup thing." *Coward.*

Katie nodded, her dark eyes pensive. Just as Zach started to say something else, she spoke again. "I called Aunt Sabrina."

"Did you?"

"Uh-huh. A while ago. When you came in here."

Zach waited, still unsure of where this conversation was going.

"Aunt Sabrina said you're sad because Miss Fairchild went home. I—I didn't know she went home." This last was said in a rush. She swallowed again. "Why did she leave? Didn't she like it here?"

Zach shrugged. "I don't know why she left, honey." That wasn't a lie. He didn't know.

For a very long moment, Katie seemed to be considering. Then she blurted out, "Was it me? She didn't like me, did she? 'Cause I was rude to her."

"Ah, Katie, it wasn't you. It was…it was a lot of things. I told you, it's complicated."

"But, Dad, I thought…you liked her a lot, didn't you?"

He nodded. "Yes. I did."

"I—I think I could like her, too. She…she was really nice to me…and we talked one time. Her dad died when she was a kid, did you know that?"

"Yes, sweetheart, I did know that," Zach said around the lump in his throat. He didn't think he could ever love his daughter more than he did at this moment.

"Then…if you told her that I…could like her…maybe she'd come back." Suddenly, her eyes filled with tears. "I don't want you to be sad anymore."

Zach got up and went over to her. A moment later, he was sitting in her chair and holding her in his arms, the same way he had when she was little. She clung to him, and he kissed the top of her head and thought how lucky he was to have a daughter like Katie.

"So what are you going to do?" Sabrina asked.

It was the next day, and Zach had asked her to have lunch with him. "What I want to do is go out to Seattle and haul her back here. The problem is, I'm not sure she'd come."

"You'll never know until you ask, will you?"

Georgie knew she had to snap out of this funk.

Today was her mother's birthday, and Harry was throwing an enormous party for her. All Harry's sons and their wives and children and stepchildren, all of Georgie's sisters and their beloveds and assorted children or children-to-be, all of Cornelia's and Harry's oldest friends, Joanna and Chick, neighbors from the old days and new days, and as many of the old gang from the early days of HuntCom as Harry could round up—all would be there.

Everyone there would be with someone.

Except Georgie.

She'd be alone, surrounded by happy couples and evidence of people in love. Even her mother had a love life!

Georgie now knew that all her earlier ideas about why she couldn't have a life with Zach were ridiculous. Her mother had been right from the beginning. She'd actually had a brilliant idea when she'd suggested Georgie might apply for the job as Zach's assistant. But even that was too late. Alex had told her yesterday he had someone in mind for the job but was waiting to see if his idea would work out before he officially announced it.

Georgie hadn't said anything. What was there to say?

She sighed heavily. She guessed she should take her shower and get ready for the party. Frankie had said she and Eli would swing by in a couple of hours and pick her up. Padding barefoot into her bedroom—Georgie rarely wore shoes at home, and thank goodness her ankle was back to normal now—she opened her closet. What should she wear?

As she was listlessly trying to decide, she heard the static-filled drone in the hallway, which meant someone was at the front door, buzzing for admittance into the building. For the dozenth time since moving in, Georgie wished they had a full-time super or guard or something—someone who could screen visitors and take care of deliveries, etc. But they didn't. This was probably the delivery Alex had mentioned yesterday. So she walked out to the hallway and pressed the intercom button. "Yes? May I help you?"

A muffled male voice said, "Delivery for Georgianna Fairchild."

"Okay. I'll buzz you in." This had to be the delivery Alex was referring to, because she was listed as G. Fairchild on the directory. Besides, she had a peephole and would not open the door if she didn't like the look of this guy. Georgie was no fool. She smiled wryly. Well, not about security, anyway.

A few minutes later, her doorbell rang. She peered through the peephole. At first all she saw was red. A second later, the red moved back and she saw that the person outside her door was a dark-haired man whose face was obscured by a huge bouquet of red roses.

"What in the world?" She squinted, looked again.

The man evidently had heard her, for he slowly lowered the bouquet and she saw his face. It was Zach. Her heart banged against her chest. *Zach!*

"Are you going to let me in, Georgie?" he called out. "I know you're in there looking at me."

Still in shock, she fumbled with the dead bolt, then the regular lock. Finally she freed the door and yanked it open. "What are you doing here?" she cried as he walked in.

"I came to say, 'Happy Valentine's Day,'" he said, holding out the roses. His blue eyes sparkled as they swept her face.

"It's not Valentine's Day," she said weakly. She was trembling and had to hold on to the little table that stood by her door.

"And 'happy birthday' and 'happy Fourth of July' and 'happy Thanksgiving' and 'merry Christmas' and

'I love you.'" His eyes had turned serious. "I love you, and I don't want to live without you."

Georgie couldn't speak. All her words were trapped in her throat. Was this really happening? Or was she dreaming it?

"Okay, if you're not going to take the flowers, I'm going to have to put them on the floor, because I want to put my arms around you." He smiled then, that smile she loved so much, the one that had been haunting her dreams. "That's if you want me to…"

"Oh, Zach," she finally managed to say, "I want that more than anything in the world."

For a long time after that, there were no more words from either one of them. Only kisses and more kisses.

"Does this mean you love me, too?" Zach asked after they finally came up for air.

"You know I do."

"I'd like to hear you say it."

She smiled. She was so happy right now. They might still have a lot of problems to solve, but at least this was a beginning. "I do love you, Zach. I think I fell in love with you the first day I saw you."

He gave her a skeptical look. "Why do I find that hard to believe?"

Georgie grinned. "Well, maybe the *second* day."

"What happened the second day?"

"You took me to your apartment and—"

"You fell in love with my *apartment?*" he said, interrupting her.

Now she laughed. "Oh, you idiot. With you! With your kids. With your life. Of course, I didn't know that then. But I do now." Then she sobered.

"I know what you're thinking about. It's Katie, isn't it?"

She sighed deeply. Nodded.

"Let me tell you about Katie," he said.

As he talked, Georgie's heart felt lighter and lighter. And when he'd finished, repeating what Katie had said about liking Georgie, Georgie's heart soared with hope.

Zach reached into the pocket of his leather jacket and withdrew a small velvet ring box. "I'm going to do this right," he said, and he got down on one knee. "Georgianna Fairchild," he said tenderly. "I love you. Will you do me the honor of becoming Mrs. Zachary Prince?" Then he opened the box.

Georgie, who didn't even like jewels, gasped when she saw the most perfect emerald-cut diamond she'd ever seen. It was a simple, elegant design of one large stone set in platinum. It was exactly the kind of ring she would have chosen herself.

As if he knew what she was thinking, he said softly, "It had your name on it."

This time, when he took her into his arms, the ring sat firmly on the ring finger of her left hand.

Two hours later, after calling Frankie and telling her she didn't need a ride, Georgie sat in the passenger seat of the Lexus Zach had rented. They were on their way to Harry's house and her mother's birthday party. Zach wore a beautifully cut dark pin-striped suit and white shirt, and Georgie wore a short, filmy red dress—in honor of the faux Valentine's Day Zach had used as a reason to bring her the red roses. Small diamond stud earrings and her new engagement ring—oh, and a smile that would not go away—were her only adornments.

"Zach," she said, "I know we're engaged, and I don't

want to change my mind, but…there's still the problem of my job. I don't want to give it up."

He smiled. "I wondered when you'd get around to that." He gave her a quick glance. "Alex has a surprise for you. He was just waiting to see if you were going to say yes or not."

"Yes about a job?"

"Yes to me when I asked you to marry me."

"You talked to Alex about me? When?"

"Yesterday."

"But I talked to Alex yesterday, and he didn't say—"

"I asked him not to."

Georgie was astounded. In another lifetime, she would have been irritated to have her boss and the man she loved talking about her behind her back. "What's the surprise?"

"It won't be a surprise if I tell you."

"Zach, I really don't like surprises."

"You liked the one today."

"Well, sometimes I make exceptions." But she laughed. She *loved* the surprise today.

"Alex is going to ask you if you want the job of co-director of the New York office." Zach smiled at her second gasp of the day. "We'll be equal in every way."

"And…you're okay with that?"

"I'm more than okay with it. It was my idea. Georgie, I want to share everything in my life with you—the good, the bad and the ugly. Isn't that what real love is all about?"

If he hadn't been driving, Georgie would have thrown her arms around him and kissed him until he cried for mercy. As it was, she contented herself with saying, "Mr. Prince, you're the man I've been waiting for all my life." Then she laughed. "My mother is going to be so happy! I can't wait to tell her she's finally going to see her holdout daughter married."

Epilogue

From the June issue of
Around Puget Sound *magazine*

Harrison Hunt Marries Again
by Phoebe Lancaster

The wedding of Harrison Hunt, founder of HuntCom, the multibillion-dollar corporation considered the grand-daddy of the personal computer industry, and Cornelia Phillips Fairchild, widow of George Fairchild, who was once Harrison Hunt's partner, took place Saturday evening at the Hunt mansion in Seattle. This is Hunt's fifth marriage and Fairchild's second.

The bride wore a full-length, pale pink lace gown designed by Vera Wang and carried white baby orchids atop an old family Bible. Mikimoto pearls adorned her neck, ears and right wrist—a wedding gift from her groom—and her spectacular pink diamond engagement ring was on full view. The groom wore a dark gray Brioni tux with a pink rose tucked into his lapel.

The bride's matron-of-honor was her oldest daughter, Georgianna "Georgie" Fairchild Prince, who recently married New Yorker Zachary Prince, one of the heirs to the McKinley textile fortune. Bridesmaids were the bride's three younger daughters: Roberta "Bobbie" Fairchild Gannon, Thomasina "Tommi" Fairchild-Callahan, both of whom are also recent brides, and Francesca "Frankie" Fairchild, who is even now planning her own summer wedding to Eli Wolf. All the beautiful Fairchild sisters wore long raspberry crepe gowns from JS Designs in Seattle.

Best man for his father was Grayson Hunt, president of HuntCom. Remaining groomsmen were Harrison Hunt's other three sons: Alex, J.T. and Justin.

After the ceremony, which was performed by the pastor of the church where Mrs. Fairchild has been a long-time member, the guests, estimated at approximately three hundred, were treated to a lavish buffet and romantic evening of dancing and multiple champagne toasts in the opulent ballroom in one wing of Hunt's spectacular lakeside home.

The new Mr. and Mrs. Harrison Hunt will spend their honeymoon in Australia and New Zealand—"Countries I've always wanted to see," according to the bride. The groom, who has admittedly not had much success with marriage in the past, smiled indulgently and said he intended to do everything in his power to please his new bride, because "she is a keeper."

* * * * *

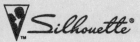
Silhouette®

COMING NEXT MONTH

Available February 22, 2011

REQUEST YOUR FREE BOOKS!

2 FREE NOVELS PLUS 2 FREE GIFTS!

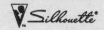

SPECIAL EDITION
Life, Love and Family!

USA TODAY *bestselling author Lynne Graham*
is back with a thrilling new trilogy
SECRETLY PREGNANT, CONVENIENTLY WED

Three heroines must marry alpha males to keep
their dreams...but Alejandro, Angelo and Cesario
are not about to be tamed!

Book 1—JEMIMA'S SECRET
Available March 2011 from Harlequin Presents®.

JEMIMA yanked open a drawer in the sideboard to find Alfie's birth certificate. Her son was her husband's child. It was a question of telling the truth whether she liked it or not. She extended the certificate to Alejandro.

"This has to be nonsense," Alejandro asserted.

"Well, if you can find some other way of explaining how I managed to give birth by that date and Alfie not be yours, I'd like to hear it," Jemima challenged.

Alejandro glanced up, golden eyes bright as blades and as dangerous. "All this proves is that you must still have been pregnant when you walked out on our marriage. It does not automatically follow that the child is mine."

"'I know it doesn't suit you to hear this news now and I really didn't want to tell you. But I can't lie to you about it. Someday Alfie may want to look you up and get acquainted."

"If what you have just told me is the truth, if that little boy does prove to be mine, it was vindictive and extremely selfish of you to leave me in ignorance!"

Jemima paled. "When I left you, I had no idea that I was still pregnant."

"Two years is a long period of time, yet you made no attempt to inform me that I might be a father. I will want DNA tests to confirm your claim before I make any decision about what I want to do."

"Do as you like," she told him curtly. "*I* know who Alfie's father is and there has never been any doubt of his identity."

"I will make arrangements for the tests to be carried out and I will see you again when the result is available," Alejandro drawled with lashings of dark Spanish masculine reserve.

"I'll contact a solicitor and start the divorce," Jemima proffered in turn.

Alejandro's eyes narrowed in a piercing scrutiny that made her uncomfortable. "It would be foolish to do anything before we have that DNA result."

"I disagree," Jemima flashed back. "I should have applied for a divorce the minute I left you!"

Alejandro quirked an ebony brow. "And why didn't you?"

Jemima dealt him a fulminating glance but said nothing, merely moving past him to open her front door in a blunt invitation for him to leave.

"I'll be in touch," he delivered on the doorstep.

What is Alejandro's next move? Perhaps rekindling their marriage is the only solution! But will Jemima agree?

Find out in Lynne Graham's
exciting new romance
JEMIMA'S SECRET

Available March 2011
from Harlequin Presents®.

Start your Best Body today with these top 3 nutrition tips!

1. SHOP THE PERIMETER OF THE GROCERY STORE: The good stuff—fruits, veggies, lean proteins and dairy—always line the outer edges of the store. When you veer into the center aisles, you enter the temptation zone, where the unhealthy foods live.

2. WATCH PORTION SIZES: Most portion sizes in restaurants are nearly twice the size of a true serving and at home, it's easy to "clean your plate." Use these easy serving guidelines:
- Protein: the palm of your hand
- Grains or Fruit: a cup of your hand
- Veggies: the palm of two open hands

3. USE THE RAINBOW RULE FOR PRODUCE: Your produce drawers should be filled with every color of fruits and vegetables. The greater the variety, the more vitamins and other nutrients you add to your diet.

Find these and many more helpful tips in

YOUR BEST BODY NOW

by

TOSCA RENO

WITH STACY BAKER

Bestselling Author of
THE EAT-CLEAN DIET

Available wherever books are sold!